PRAISE FROM MORE BY

JAMES CASPER

Outstanding book. One of the best novels I've ever read. Would like to read more by this author.

— LAYTON LUNDON

Thank you, Mr. Casper. It feels as if you wrote this story for me. Your characters are lovely…a breath of fresh air. You made me laugh and you sure made me cry.

— PATRICIA POLK

It's such a tightly woven story – I love that about it. All the characters, backstories, plot twists…it all comes together so beautifully.

— SS

LINES THAT DO NOT CROSS

MINNESOTA STORIES

JAMES CASPER

Edited by
KATE CASPER
and
RACHEL WHY

FARHAVEN PRESS

Front Cover: A double exposure by the author included here to demonstrate that when things go wrong, you wind up with a good story.

Something needs to go wrong for a story to develop. Sometimes things get straightened out in the storytelling and sometimes they don't. Either way, it gives one something to think about.

Photo of the early 19th century railroad trestle that once spanned Shingobee Bay of Leech Lake, Minnesota.

ISBN: 978-0-9994715-9-3

*In grateful memory of Dr. Edward Sarmiento, mentor
and friend, who encouraged my writing*

CONTENTS

FOREWORD

Lines That Do Not Cross, a lovely collection of stories by James Casper, quietly weaves together a cross section of nostalgia with family dynamics. It is interlaced with humor as well as an endearing regard for humanity. The spectrum of characters we encounter ranges from hopeful dreamers and restless souls to those lost to an ideal that has no place in the modern world—and then there's a very special dog.

We begin with the adventures of a retired couple, the Tuttles, whose love of northern Minnesota causes them to make some decisions regarding their retirement years which are, in retrospect, ill advised. "Somewhere North of Northome" is a dreamy depiction of the ideal versus reality and how the very climate over-whelms them in ways that come as no surprise to anyone familiar with this part of the United States. As their various friends retire to the warmth of Arizona, the Tuttles follow their hearts, inspired by the lovely summers they experienced in Minnesota, a choice that soon haunts them.

"Benjamin's Gift" tells of another kind of haunting, a chronic nagging that the best in life is gone forever. Benjamin, a farmer with a wife and three children, isolates himself in the staunch belief that his old ways are infinitely superior to the changes the modern world is bringing to his household. As his longing for the past increases, so does his disgust with everyone he encounters, and the results prove disastrous. I wondered a lot about Benjamin and his world view. Is he correct that "nothing's like it used to be"? In many ways he is, but whilst the reader may feel there are many solutions to his problems, his hopelessness and anger prove to be a detriment, causing the suffering of the innocents around him. This is a cautionary tale, one that warns of the dangers of sentimentality and an inability to adjust to change which is, of course, the only true constant in life.

Change comes rapidly to Danny Harp and his family when his father returns from the war. "A Child of the War" follows a young boy growing up within a loving family until they are all tested as Johnny Harp grapples with the demons he has brought home. The fear of Johnny's erratic moods permeate every aspect of their daily lives, and the unpredictability leaves an everlasting mark. I found Danny to be an inspiring young man, finding ways to navigate through a life filled with uncertainty.

We meet another inspiring young man in "The Far End of the Park." Jude is a sweet and quiet soul who lives with his mother in a cabin on a summer resort. They are the caretakers of the park in the off season. Their isolation leads to a subsequent fascination with the park's other resident, Miss Thorpe. Long before she and Jude meet face to face, her beautiful singing voice becomes a comfort to Jude, providing a haunting backdrop and a hopefulness in a lonely young man's life.

We encounter Jude again thanks to the efforts of George Cobb, a well-meaning gentleman who decides that perhaps a dog would be a great benefit to the lonely young man in "And the Dog Came Back." This special animal and its owner take center stage in a story of goodwill which backfires with unintentionally hilarious results. The dog, for a while named Floyd, takes George on a chaotic and expensive mini adventure that gets out of control, bordering on slapstick.

This thoughtful collection of stories is filled with memorable characters and beautiful imagery. The author's ability to take the reader into his characters' lives through exquisite and insightful detail, while occasionally adding a delightful sense of humor, makes this an engaging body of work. It has been a privilege to read!

Rachel Why, Editor

SOMEWHERE NORTH OF NORTHOME

*M*r. and Mrs. Tuttle were about ready to retire. The past four summers, they left their Chicago business in the care of a son-in-law while they vacationed in northern Minnesota. Each year, the couple lingered later into August as Mr. Tuttle made the twin discoveries of an early northern autumn and a business that went forward without him.

The first two summers, they rented a cabin at Happy Bay Resort, a lodge and six pine-sided cabins on a small sand-bottom lake. Mr. Tuttle found it highly rated in his credit card directory, and at the time, it seemed a sensible thing. They were newcomers to the north and needed the guidance of people like the Wentworths who ran their resort as though city dwellers should have a paternal introduction to so many pine trees and lakes.

"You mustn't fear the wilderness," Mrs. Wentworth often told Mrs. Tuttle in those days. "Go out to it, and you will find peace in your lives."

Mrs. Wentworth had evangelistic ways, and growing more intimate with the Tuttles during their second summer, she once confessed her desire to be cremated, with her ashes flung from a plane over the Superior National Forest.

Mrs. Tuttle had often gone with Mr. Tuttle, following a series of excursions the Wentworths planned for them, never taking them farther than a half-day's drive from Happy Bay Resort. They always arrived home before sunset where they could sit on deck chairs in front of their cabin and await the first loon's cry.

"There now, isn't this the life?" Mr. Tuttle would sometimes say as he settled into the taut fabric of his chair.

Mrs. Tuttle could not but agree, and she wept when they moved out of Happy Bay Resort after their second summer. She embraced Mrs. Wentworth, and then Mrs. Wentowrth wept. Mr Tuttle arranged with Mr. Wentworth to rent another season. They shook hands, and the Wentworths stood outside their lodge waving as the Tuttles drove away.

"It's just like leaving home," Mrs. Tuttle said between sobs, and Mr. Tuttle nodded as he turned onto the highway and accelerated. It began raining after they crossed the south Wisconsin border. East of Elgin, Illinois, Mrs. Tuttle peered out through their smeared windshield and declared, "The city is becoming a jungle."

Two things altered the Tuttles' plan over the winter. Mr. Tuttle discovered that Happy Bay Resort had fallen in the opinion of his new credit card directory, and a recently widowed friend of Mrs. Tuttle offered to sell her husband's travel trailer at an enormous saving.

The following summer they pulled their trailer into northern Minnesota, carefully avoiding the route past Happy Bay Resort. Alone, they explored strange lakeshores and new vistas of poplar and white pine.

They learned they no longer needed the Wentworths, forgetting as well that they ever needed them at all. They sat in orange lawn chairs beside their trailer, awaiting the loon's cry over Upper Red Lake.

"There were mice in the Wentworth's cabins," Mrs. Tuttle said.

Another summer followed like this. They rented a lot for their trailer on the banks of the Tamarack River just a mile upstream from Red Lake. Mr. Tuttle bought a fishing rod, a plastic tackle box, a rainbow assortment of lures. Mrs. Tuttle brought her geraniums from Chicago, planting them in front of the trailer where they thrived in the warm sun of long, northern days.

"Now it's just like home," she said.

August came, and the dense foliage of riverside thickets began to brown slightly underneath. In ditches and further up on the river banks, grass was turning red and brown.

"I never knew the dominant ground color of late summer was red," Mr. Tuttle said.

The evenings were cool, and before they returned to Chicago from their fourth northern summer, Mrs. Tuttle had potted her geraniums again and carried them inside from the first frost.

That winter in Chicago, all their friends seemed to be retiring and moving away to Florida or New Mexico. Mrs. Tuttle's widow friend remarried, sold her house, and leased another in Orlando.

"We like the north country," Mrs. Tuttle said. "We have peace in the wilderness," she said.

Mr. Tuttle agreed, and they talked of retiring to northern Minnesota.

"I do not think we are as old as the others anymore," he said, referring to their Chicago friends who, each winter, went south like the birds, and now, unlike the birds, were staying there. "I think it has something to do with living in the north. I read somewhere that inhabitants of torrid climates age more quickly."

Mr. Tuttle, a trim sixty-eight years, had clean, brown eyes, a full head of gray, wavy hair, and precisely trimmed mustache. He felt ten years younger and more than kept up with his 50-something wife who struggled with lifting heavy loads of wash lately.

A storm brought twenty inches of snow to Chicago that January. It was cold for a day or two afterwards, and then, when the wind shifted south, the snow turned to ashen slop. Mr. Tuttle thought he saw a moral in this. "We live in two worlds," he said. "Snow in the north country would be white and clean the winter through."

Though he had never seen it, he was sure, and, for a week or two, while the dirty Chicago snow melted into the sewers, he stayed inside, leaving business to his son-in-law and contemplating the rainbow fishing lures he often set out on the dining room table.

When they went north for their fifth summer, Mr. Tuttle said, "I have to keep a hand in somewhere."

He had now transferred the family business to his son-in-law, reserving only a share in its profits, and he was thinking of a small store they sometimes patronized in the remote back country near the lake.

It was a store that sold mostly loaves of bread, cartons of eggs, milk, coffee, and fishing licenses to vacationers who thought it not worth a thirty-mile trip to buy these things at a lower price in town. It was set off by itself where two narrow gravel roads intersected in an area of lakeshore marsh and tamarack groves. He had become acquainted with its owners the year before and knew they were thinking of selling out.

"It wouldn't bother us a bit to run that store," Mr. Tuttle told his wife a dozen times during their trip north.

It was early May, the soonest they had ever come. When they crossed the Continental Divide, poplar leaves were their momentary golden green, and red oak was only budding.

"The rivers from here flow north to Hudson Bay," Mr. Tuttle said. "We have left the Mississippi system."

Water from melting snow ran high in road-side ditches. Several times they stopped to watch mallards swimming in pairs through frail, young marsh grass. Mr. Tuttle kept his binoculars un-cased in the front seat, and once, when they parked to view some turtles sunning on a willow log, a great blue heron rose out of the reeds nearby. They could see water draining from its legs. One by one, the turtles slipped into the cold, blue water.

"Spring is the season of life," Mr. Tuttle said, trying to follow the heron's flight with his binoculars.

Mrs. Tuttle could not have agreed more, but she wondered then why she should be noticing how white her husband's hair had become.

Unawares, they drove directly past Happy Bay Resort and without going first to their lot by the river, they stopped at the store.

When they got out of the car, the young marsh grass was brilliant green for miles around. Tamarack bloomed, a dozen birds in every tree, and between the trees, dozens more were flying.

Mr. Tuttle bent behind his car to check his

trailer hitch. He could hear water gurgling through a culvert beneath the road. When he stood up to face the store, he saw a FOR SALE sign in its front window. It seemed to spin around, as though he were looking at it from a carnival ride. Mrs. Tuttle thought his face was a deathly white.

"I only stood up too quickly," he said.

Because they could not have the store till September, they spent another summer in their travel trailer by the river. In early May, without the crowds of tourists they had always associated with the north country, they felt uneasy, a sense of abandonment.

They noticed that the wind through so many trees took on a lonely whine. They discovered the heavy, angular shadows the spring sun can cast through an empty roadside park. At night in their travel trailer, while Mr. Tuttle slept, Mrs. Tuttle thought she could hear the river rushing in high water through grass along the bank.

She closed her eyes, feeling herself swept along in its current, helpless as a stick and not knowing where it might take her.

They awoke one morning to a three-inch snowfall, but the sun broke through by noon, the snow melted, and beneath that, the grass was somehow greener yet.

The parks and campgrounds gradually filled with tourists, and they set aside their fears.

Mrs. Tuttle put out her potted geraniums in June. Mr. Tuttle bought a dozen new fishing lures. In July, when the geraniums were blooming and fish quit biting, they returned to Chicago for a week.

There was furniture to sell and give away. There was furniture to prepare for the movers. There were old friends to see for a last time, perhaps.

They had a retirement party in a large, downtown hotel. They invited everyone to their store in the north, and most of them promised to come sometime.

"We're going to remodel the living quarters in our store," Mr. Tuttle said. "We'll have guest rooms, and there'll always be plenty of groceries."

Their friends laughed, their daughter and son-in-law laughed, and the morning after the party, Mr. Tuttle felt a trembling in his chest.

They returned to the north where, in August, they put their trailer up for sale, and Mrs. Tuttle potted her geraniums as protection against the early frost she had learned to expect. But August was warm and dry that year, and the sumac turned red from drought instead.

In September, they moved into the store with their furniture and geraniums. A week later, they watched their travel trailer roll away for Milwaukee with new tenants aboard.

"It was just like home," Mrs. Tuttle said, suppressing a sob.

"It's no use running the store till we're settled," Mr. Tuttle said. He nailed a CLOSED sign to the front door, missing the nail and blackening his thumb in the process.

He told the bread man, the milk man, and the wholesale grocer's man not to stop for a few weeks. Mr. Tuttle had money enough to do without his store completely. It would be his hobby for the winter months and quiet times in the summer. He thought he could bring out groceries and sundries like a stamp collection whenever he felt bored.

After Labor Day the crowds of tourists dwindled, but with the hammering and sawing and tracking back and forth of two carpenters they hired to remodel their living quarters, Mr. And Mrs. Tuttle hardly noticed at first.

Mr. Tuttle had the carpenters make window boxes for his wife's geraniums, and he busied himself cleaning up outside. His thumb was swollen and healing slowly, but he gradually formed a pile of tin cans and rubbish, and he hired a truck to haul it away along with some rotting logs and a spool of rusty barbed wire.

He raked the leaves that blew from a poplar in their yard. An outhouse stood to one side of their store for customers' use, and he painted it inside and out. He worked through successions of bright autumn days, an hour or two at a time. The work was harder than he thought it would be, and he felt at times like a tired man making his way through a big book, one page, another, and then no more for this day.

The poplar leaves were gold in falling and brown before he could rake them away. October came, but Mr. Tuttle kept the store closed because he had had more dizzy spells.

The carpenters finished their work and left. A week of cold rain at last ripped every leaf from the poplars in their yard. Out in the marshland all around them, frost had killed the lush summer grasses. Cattails and tamarack were turning brown.

Only this year had Mrs. Tuttle learned about the tamaracks. "Here is one coniferous tree that sheds its foliage," Mr. Tuttle had informed her on their trip north that spring, and at the time, with all the tamarack turning green, she didn't mind, but now she wasn't sure she liked the idea.

She peered from her kitchen window in a back room of their darkened store. Everything around her seemed to be dying. She studied the browning grass and tamarack needles, the bare skeletons of their yard trees.

There were hardly any birds left, and she could hear the wind moan as it had before in early May. She looked up and down the gravel road running by her window. Only once or twice a day, a car came past, and since the store was closed, it never stopped.

On both sides now, the road was blending into the brown marshland as if it would disappear, leaving them cut off altogether.

"How far is it to our neighbors, John?" she asked.

"About five miles," Mr. Tuttle said.

She thought he mumbled.

October was gone. The days grew noticeably shorter. The sun was low in the sky all day, even at noon casting long shadows through their yard.

Mrs. Tuttle moved her geraniums to a south window, but they continued to fade. Their blossoms browned at the edges, opened wide, and disintegrated, falling petal by petal to the windowsill. Each morning, Mrs. Tuttle brushed them into her hand where they lay curled up and softly dead in the dry landscape of her palm.

One night in mid-November, they were awakened by the chatter of ice crystals against their bedroom window. Mr. Tuttle got up and looked outside.

"It's storming," he whispered when he returned to bed.

Mrs. Tuttle awoke in the morning without Mr. Tuttle at her side. She lay in bed listening for the sound of him moving around in other rooms, but the store was quiet, save for its tortuous creaking in the northeast wind, the dripping of a bathroom faucet, the rhythmical banging of a stovepipe draft.

Mrs. Tuttle peered from her bedroom window. The landscape in gray morning light was ashen white as far as she could see. Snow blew diagonally out of the featureless slate clouds, forming in the wind, drifts, like waves across their yard.

In the driveway beyond some cedar shrubs

where the drifts were deepest, Mr. Tuttle bent over his shovel, cleaning a path from their garage to the road that had first brought them here so many carefree months ago.

What was he thinking? The snow filled in behind him as fast as he toiled through it, and while Mrs. Tuttle watched, his shovel moved back and forth more slowly.

Her breath fogged the window glass and, twice, she wiped it with her nightgown. Then she ran to the back door where she called to him.

"John," she shouted in a voice the wind seemed to wrench from her. Snow struck her in the face and curled around her bare ankles. She could see her husband's arms faltering among the drifts like a springwound child's toy slowing to a stop. "John," she called again.

He raised one hand in what seemed a limp gesture of farewell, and then she lost sight of him behind the snow and cedar shrubbery.

She found him sitting in a drift. His eyes were open, snow piled on his lashes. The shovel lay across his lap, and a pointed drift was already forming behind him. Struggling against the rising and falling winds, they staggered together into the store. Moments later, with him in bed, she sat by his side, holding for him a shot of brandy he attempted to sip.

"I'm all right," he murmured. "Only another dizzy spell."

But Mrs. Tuttle thought his voice was weak and far away from her. She felt his hand under the covers. In the gray light at their window, their limits came upon her with grim formality. She felt helpless and regretful.

She might have said to him at that moment, "John. We should have known this would happen." Her voice, though, barricaded within her, felt weak, trembly, like his hand.

With Mr. Tuttle sleeping and breathing more regularly, she gathered her thoughts about her like the sweater she buttoned to her chin. She made some coffee, spilling it in the saucer as she tried to drink it. She thought of the lakeshore lot where they first parked their trailer for the summer. She thought of the spring river swollen with melted snow, the blooming cattails, the cry of the loon in summer twilights. She thought of the Wentworths and Happy Bay Resort.

Go out to the wilderness and find peace, Mrs. Wentworth had said.

Mrs. Tuttle considered this and no longer could locate the truth in it.

Do not be afraid, Mrs. Wentworth had said, but her assurance lay like dead leaves and grass beneath the snow.

Mrs. Tuttle went to the bedroom for her husband's brandy glass and finished what he had left. She studied him sleeping with his back to her, her thoughts wandering away with their car on the home trip to Chicago after each of their summers in the north. Was this the man who drove and did not lose his way?

She left his brandy glass on the nightstand.

Returning to the kitchen, she tried to recall the numbers of road signs marking their way back. But something new lay in that direction.

Mr. Tuttle knew. Cradled in his sleeping brain were the numbers 71 and 2, then the Interstate from Duluth to Madison, Wisconsin. Mrs. Tuttle tried to imagine these signs, green and white reflectorized. In the headlights of their car, they boomed out of the roadside darkness. She read each of them in turn, but they were to her algebraic and abstract, a mysterious equation which, in her fear and confusion, directed her thoughts to the Wentworth's resort instead of Chicago.

She put on her coat and scarf, a pair of boots and gloves that belonged to Mr. Tuttle and almost fit her. She stepped outside into the storm where her world had become white from one horizon to another, its throbbing dimensions seeming to swell and shrink as the wind rose and fell. The brown marsh grass, the bare tamarack and poplar, the roads running both ways past their store—these were all white as if intent on hiding from her.

She trudged through the drifts to the crossroad, looking for a sign of hope or some assurance, now as muffled and obscure as everything around her. Surely, John must have had this in mind when he set out with the shovel, now nowhere to be found.

Then she remembered something John had shared recently. One of the carpenters building her window boxes told him that settlers used to tie ropes between buildings so they wouldn't lose their way in a blizzard. John chuckled as he relayed the tale. *"I told him about Chicago snows and Lake Michigan and not being able to see across the street."* He chuckled again.

She was without a rope where there were no streets.

She looked back toward the store, but it was lost beyond a pulsating veil. Nothing could have been as dark and bewildering as a world this white. She stared all directions. The swirling landscape revealed nothing about what was front or back or to either side.

She spun like a child, twirling in the wind with eyes closed. Somewhere out there was John and their dreams.

She knew they would never get back.

BENJAMIN'S GIFT

*J*ohn Walter was the oldest of Benjamin's three sons, and on his twelfth birthday, Benjamin gave him his first gun, a squirrel rifle in a brown canvas case. Afterwards, as they ate John Walter's cake with pink ice cream scooped on top, Benjamin told them about his own father giving him his first gun.

It wasn't a long story, but he made it that way because he spoke as he chewed, with the slow, halting movements of a man who looked for the seed of some fruit he was eating. The boys were shifting in their chairs and punching each other before he finished. His wife Grace circled the table, gathering plates and forks into a plastic dishpan. When Benjamin looked up from his story, he knew nobody had listened.

It was too late that evening to try the gun. The sun had fallen into a crimson blaze of autumn dust, and above that, the brighter stars were glimmering in the chill October air. There was no light for them to shoot by, and Benjamin had yet to milk his cows. Thus was John Walter given a whole day to think about his first gun, a day for his excitement to grow.

The next morning, with the sun flaming through the barren tops of distant trees and evening fogs still clinging to pasture hollows, Benjamin was milking his cows again. John Walter and his brothers ate breakfast and waited for their school bus. This morning, it came with a tawny cloud of dust trailing in the air far behind it and drifting away slowly over the dried and bent corn rows. Its folding doors sprang open for his sons who climbed in one by one, without waving or even so much as looking aside to see their father standing there.

Benjamin stood in his barn doorway watching the bus back over the thin, angular shadow of his windmill, always a shadow on the ground, morning and afternoon—until the bus was there

—and then for a moment it lay like a drooping flower over its long, yellow roof.

When the door opened, Benjamin could hear the high-pitched chatter, the shrill screams of fifty children, sounding remote and beyond him like the distant cries of wild geese. Then he heard the drone of a radio the driver was playing, and finally the doors snapped shut.

The bus moved off down the driveway with small, white faces peering through the dusty glass of its rear windows, staring at him. Benjamin stared back without knowing any of them. A hand waved at him. Another stuck up a finger.

Benjamin turned away, his face burning. Above him, the old windmill began its slow, screeching turn in a shifting morning breeze. He gazed up at it, wondering absently why he hadn't torn it down, why it hadn't fallen down long ago of its own accord. He liked windmills, but there didn't seem to be any place for them these days.

His own pumped idly away in every wind, futilely raising and lowering a disconnected rod, thrusting away at nothing, accomplishing nothing in its ancient, rusting vigor, while its blue tin paddles circled overhead like the sun and stars above them. These days an electric motor worked the pump.

Benjamin lowered his eyes and went into the barn. The school bus was shifting gears on the county road.

At four o'clock, it returned with his sons, and an hour later, Benjamin came up from the back pasture where he had worked the afternoon mending fences. His cows had moved ahead of him and were in a black and white huddle behind the barn. It was one of those bland autumn afternoons of featureless gray clouds and suddenly faded colors, when the mask slips from the golden birch, the ruddy maple, and the honey grass.

The world seemed weary of itself. Benjamin felt weary. The ground beneath his feet had become an old rug. He put his hammer, wire cutters, and a paper sack of staples on a bench in his tool shed, all the while thinking of John Walter and the new rifle they should have time to try this afternoon. On his way to the house, he rummaged through a trash pile for six rusty cans, and before he went in, he arranged them on a backyard fence facing out over his cornfields.

As he sat in a corner of the living room, cleaning and oiling the new gun, a gray wash of sky seemed to deepen at the windows. It was the sky of an autumn day gone cloudy with the promise of snow.

At Benjamin's side on a limed-oak coffee table reposed a vase of plastic marigolds. John Walter and his brothers were sitting across the room on the carpet watching television. He wondered why the boy wasn't standing at his side instead, watching him swab the barrel, inside and out, feeling with his boyish hands the slender brass shells lined up in a row of six on the table.

He recalled again when he was a boy with his first rifle, not a new one like this, but an old single-shot with a bent sight, cracked stock, and broken trigger tip. His father had given it to him and said, "This is yours to shoot with." It wasn't in a canvas case either. It wasn't his birthday. His father just passed it to him, laying it across his open hands.

Benjamin could remember how it felt at first, lying there, heavier than he imagined a real gun would be, but not so heavy that he couldn't raise it to his shoulder and take a steady aim. Its old hickory stock was rough in places where other hunters had carried it over fences, leaned it against trees, or hauled it in the back of some truck jolting across a meadow. It was worn bare of varnish, and its barrel didn't gleam at all like the one he bought for John Walter. But John Walter was on the floor focused on the television.

As he shifted the gun from one side to the other, its butt brushed against the plastic marigolds. The stiff bouquet toppled over, not the way real flowers fall in the careless disarray of light and living things, but like a mannequin. Benjamin struggled to get the arrangement to stand on the table again.

He had never liked plastic flowers. He didn't like plastic ducks on their front lawn. He was a farmer, and at times in the fall and winter, a hunter. There were real ducks now moving into the marshland south of his farm by the river. In his fields there was corn, brown and ragged from early frosts, waiting to be harvested. There were cows in the barn to be milked after supper.

Grace, on the other hand, had an enduring fascination for the counterfeit. She kept plastic flowers throughout their house in cold, perpetual bloom: pansies atop the refrigerator, a rose arrangement behind glass in a china cabinet for thirteen years since their wedding, even some Sweet Williams on the toilet tank, not to mention the marigolds which had been around since early summer.

Grace had bought them for the family plot,

and now four months had come and gone without her getting them to the cemetery.

Grace came in without saying a word and sat beside the boys on their "Hide-a-Bed" couch. Benjamin glanced toward the kitchen as he ran an oil rag over the gun barrel. He wondered what was happening to supper. On the television screen, a man in a lavender suitcoat was smiling with dazzling teeth while he pointed to a scoreboard where numbers flashed in green and blue and red lights behind a panel of children contestants.

It was a color set, a six-hundred-dollar television Benjamin had bought last Christmas at Grace's insistence. She argued that it wouldn't cost any more than if they bought presents for everybody, and instead, they would just have the television as one present for the whole family. It had been about the only present last Christmas, too, except for a pair of socks under their artificial tree from his Uncle Milton and three plastic dart guns sent along in the same box for the boys. They had opened Uncle Milton's present right after supper and spent the rest of the evening watching television. All except Benjamin, that is.

He had gone out to the barn to milk his cows and then was called back to the house by Grace's screams. The television's color wasn't right, and through Christmas Eve, all of Christmas Day, and much of his spare time since, he had been trying to adjust it.

The first time he bent over to turn a knob, one of the boys shot him with a dart. They laughed, Benjamin swore, and Grace said that his bad temper was ruining Christmas. He bent over the set again and again after that, but its color never was like the real color, and it washed like running dye all over the screen.

Even today, with everything Benjamin tried to adjust the color, the man with a lavender coat had a lavender face to match.

He was asking a blue-faced girl what was the capital of France. She smiled serenely in front of that wall of flashing, colored lights. She showed her teeth, parting her lips slightly in the practiced happiness of a beauty queen. But her face struck Benjamin as cold and rubbery, as though passed from the same mold as those peering at him from the bus windows this morning. The girl kept smiling, the man in the lavender coat kept smiling, but she either didn't know the answer or was trying to make work out of it.

John Walter looked up from the screen and

shouted at his father, "What's the capital of France?"

Benjamin opened his mouth. "Paris."

Grace glared at him.

"Paris," the girl on the screen said almost simultaneously.

"Paris is right," the man in the lavender coat shrieked.

An unseen audience cheered, colored lights flashed, John Walter clapped his hands. Grace's face wore the smug look of a woman who had two more years of school than her husband.

Benjamin thought he smelled smoke drifting in from the kitchen. The man in the lavender coat was asking another question. John Walter was still sitting on the floor instead of standing by his side. He was swabbing the gun carefully.

A friend of his in the store where he bought it told him to clean a new gun before using it. "You never know how they come from the factory these days," he cautioned. "There might be something left in the barrel. It's best to clean them. Nothing's like it used to be."

Benjamin thought about that. "It's true," he said to himself. "Nothing's like it used to be."

He had known it for a long time now. It was possible to avoid the fact sometimes where certain things were concerned. A cow was still a cow, a barn a barn, and if you took care of the cow, she gave you milk. The leaves still fell in the autumn and new ones grew each spring, but somehow, this dreary afternoon, his friend's idea was there more certainly than ever. *Nothing's like it used to be.* It dulled every leaf, it grayed the sky, and lay upon the grass.

Twenty years ago when Benjamin was a boy, not long after his father had given him the gun, he came home another day with a television, an enormous box of a set with a small, round screen in the center like a dimple. Life began to change after that. No one sat in the living room and talked after supper anymore. They all watched Roller Derby instead.

They checked everyone's eyes twice at school those years. Some people heard that television could make you blind. He remembered traveling to this Uncle Milton's house for Easter. A bigger set was there for them to watch, and he hadn't been in front of it a minute before Uncle Milton put a pair of sunglasses on him.

"Watch your eyes," he said. "Don't sit close."

And then a dozen of them sat there all Easter afternoon—with a warm sun outside and violets blooming beneath the trees—watching television through a dozen pairs of colored glasses Uncle Milton kept in a shoebox beside his set. They had become a band of beach bathers, huddled on the sand beneath an awning. The world before them was diminished to a glowing, twenty-inch square, forever smaller and farther away.

He thought about the old pub in town where a man couldn't talk with his friends anymore because an enormous television was installed high up in a corner to one side of the bar. It was always on louder than anyone could talk, and if you tried to talk that loud, somebody just turned the set up a bit.

He thought about a New Year's Day he had failed to hunt rabbits with his father and a few of his father's friends, the first he could remember they hadn't gone out hunting in the snow.

He thought again about John Walter sitting there on the floor watching the screen, not standing beside him intent on his new gun. He stared into the dazzling mouth of the man with a lavender coat, and as he did, things were beginning to form in his mind.

He heard Grace call out the next answer. He heard the audience roar and saw the colored lights flash. He imagined a lifetime of autumns blowing leaves over the dry, honey lawn. And every tumbling, skipping leaf bore the face of the lavender man.

From the kitchen he could smell something burning for sure now. Faint smoke was curling onto the ceiling. The off-putting scent was just a part of everything in the air around him and reminding him of how things had changed.

He thought about rubber-faced children giving him the finger, his own sons shooting him with plastic darts, a Christmas without presents. He thought about Sweet Williams in their bathroom and the plastic marigolds blooming for a hundred years once they got out to the cemetery.

He knew he could be sure what he hit with a .22 rifle from fifteen feet, and whatever danger there might be, they'd all be better off for it.

There were five shells standing in a row beneath the plastic marigolds, and the man in the lavender suitcoat was still smiling when the gun went off and the colored lights went out on an autumn afternoon in Benjamin's house.

A CHILD OF THE WAR

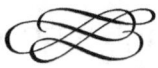

*P*hotos of Danny Harp growing up in the decade after the Second World War have in common his weak right eye, whose sensitivity to light became especially evident when he was posed in bright sun for family snapshots. In dozens such, the boy squints and twists his head, throwing his weak eye into shadow and his features into tortured profile.

"Daniel, don't make such a face," his mother would sometimes coax from the shadows.

She never herself took the pictures, needing no family reminders, wanting none apparently in a life too crowded for sentimental furniture. Usually it was Uncle Emery, her older brother, peering into the viewer of a box camera held waist high. He would shift his whole body on the balls of his feet in an odd swaying dance to admit or exclude from the record sections of weathered porch railing and picket fence, hens scratching in the daylily beds, and his own long shadow. Emery noted the leghorns but ignored the boy's contortions. The pleas of Danny's mother unavailing, his face was recorded as the sun left it.

His First Communion picture is like this. Emery trotted him out to the brightest spot in the yard, stood him at attention facing the sun, and shot him dressed in brilliant white, with a white tie tied too short, one eye wide open and watering, the other clamped shut, and his mouth shaped as if from the hopeless effort to put his tongue in his ear. It's a terrible picture, an embarrassment, and it reminds Danny of another old shame, the trauma of his first confession, a week before, in St. Barnaby's Church adjacent St. Barnaby's School. He was seven and Pius XII was pope.

Along with his twenty classmates, he had been drilled in the penitential routine by Sister Mary Florence, a novice nun with boot-camp ways. This culminated on a Thursday morning in middle May when she marched them on a broken flagstone pathway through the cemetery between school and church and then into pews along the right church aisle—things had a perverse way of showing up on Danny's weak side.

They knelt before a brilliantly painted Saint Barnaby, first martyr, a three-foot-high statue upon an ivory pedestal flanked by flickering red and white vigil lights. Barnaby wore a congenial look belying he'd been stoned to death, a fate Sister Mary Florence had seemed to relish in her account of it.

But the effigy to wrench a boy's heart stood higher up and withdrawn into a gloomy niche over Barnaby's left shoulder. St. Joseph, whom one might have thought a jovial carpenter, seemed to have just struck his thumb with a hammer and to be casting about for someone to blame. His dark gaze appeared fixed upon Danny, and Danny returning it, momentarily wondered what on earth he had done wrong and what he would say when his turn came to enter the confessional.

He would have to say something.

Lowering his eyes, he groped mentally for Mary Florence's instructions. They were never far from his thoughts. Even the slowest of his classmates knew them by heart.

The hitch was that her directives led like a

military truck convoy straight into the stone wall of sin and guilt.

His catechism provided a list of sins, but the important sounding ones weren't *his* sins. Whatever his teacher said about idolatry, calumny, adultery, and the like brought them no closer to his life. He wasn't supposed to worship a golden calf. If he lived in a glass house, he shouldn't throw stones. Boys shouldn't touch girls below their noses. Girls shouldn't touch boys below theirs. A classmate of his, one of the St. Barnaby town kids, had suggested to him at recess that if girls just stood on their heads, everything would be all right.

And guilt he didn't understand at all. Mary Florence's directives had no underpinning of lengthy explanation when there was ritual to per-form, so, fold your hands, cross your thumbs, and be sure to point your fingers straight toward heaven.

Bow down, fall on your knees, confess!

"Confess what?" Had he raised his hand to ask, Mary Florence would have rolled her eyes in amazement.

Danny rehearsed his memorized prayers.

He tried examining his conscience as he had

been taught, looking for this "honest voice" inside himself who knew what he had done.

That was how his teacher put it, but his effort turned at once into a chase after something adrift enigmatically and aimlessly through his mind, winking among shrubs and moon shadows, like a firefly on a summer's night. Just as he got close enough to catch it, it would dim to nothing and drift away.

What if girls were standing on their heads? What then would he confess?

Meanwhile Mary Florence's other little soldiers marched according to her plan. Others ahead of him in the pew row were standing up and moving toward the confessional, stepping in unison toward lines formed on either side. As soon as one came out the next went in.

An all but inaudible hum came from the little curtained rooms where they knelt behind purple drapes with the priest between them behind a door. They had all been warned not to eavesdrop, so mixed in with Danny's effort to think of a sin was the effort *not* to hear something that might have helped him if he could simply have said what somebody ahead of him said.

Wood slid against wood as the priest worked a small door to bring into view and close out with forgiveness the tiny faces appearing either side of him. In the pew ahead of Danny, penance prayers were already being said. Beneath St. Barnaby, flames danced in the glass lights. St. Joseph glowered and seemed to lean out of his niche. Danny squirmed and rose from his pew.

For relief as he stood in line, he turned to nearby wall plaques, tiny bronze plates designating sections of stained-glass window purchased by families to commemorate their dead. A wave of reverence gripped him, and he did what the nearest of them asked.

He prayed for *the soul of Annie O'Neal, beloved daughter of Thomas and Beatrice.*

The line in front of him melted away. Still without an important sin, he flung himself on his knees in the dark other side of the confessional drapes. He swallowed hard and thought his heart would choke him when his turn came to speak.

"And what do you have to tell me?" asked the priest responding to a stifled gasp.

"Adultery—six times, Father," Danny squeaked. And then, when it seemed too terrible to implicate others in this desperate revelation, he croaked, "Alone."

"*Alone* you say?" the astonished priest had asked.

"Alone," a suddenly more confident Danny repeated. Somewhere out in a moonlit yard his firefly conscience winked approvingly, then drifted away. Danny could have swooned with relief. He didn't know what he had confessed, but it was enough to get him through, and he wasn't expected to say much more.

"Is that all, my boy?"

"All, Father."

But it never would be quite all...

Thereafter, between confessions, Danny collected sins like a birdwatcher building his field list. Fights with brothers and sisters, fibs, missed church on Sunday—these were the common flock, his sparrows, starlings, and hopping lawn robins. With such in hand, he had no further need for *adultery*, an exotic southern bird with brilliant feathers and a huge bill, seldom seen in the north where he lived.

He often missed Sunday church because no one in his family dared ask his father for the required ride to town. Johnny Harp was a reverent man in the paroxysms of his wild melancholy. Out along the lurching pendulum swings of his moods lay tiny arcs where worship was possible, at least for others. Only then did he ferry his wife and four children to church and pick them up afterwards, a five-mile roundtrip in his wreck of a car with gravel dust smoking through its floorboard holes as they rocketed along.

Danny, the eldest, and Jack and Eileen sat in back coughing up pieces of Clay County. Mary, the baby, bounced along up front between her parents. Johnny Harp's notion of driving was acceleration no matter what road, what weather, what the condition of his car, the state of his mind, or the number of his family with him. Weather and family were variables increasing the risk, but the road to St. Barnaby's was always a washboard, his car always a jalopy, his mind a fire, and only with death squarely in front of him —mere yards away—would he lift his foot from the accelerator.

Any Sunday morning his brakes failed could have been the last for them all.

St. Barnaby's plated church spire and the town water tower lurched into view over a vista of frolicking corn tassels. From the old car—leaping and bounding over bumps, rattling and shimmying—the countryside really did seem to dance. Not a waltz, either, but a whirling, hopping, peasant jig of farm houses in circles of dancing trees. Cows danced with their noses in dewy pasture grass, electric poles hopped by in a blur, and a ringlet jiggled from the back of Mary's head.

If Johnny's car did seventy full throttle, they were doing seventy, if ninety without exploding, then they were doing ninety when they reached the tar flat on the outskirts of town where the world either side of them became at once a river sliding smoothly by. The white balustrades of houses, boulevards of prairie cottonwoods, and frame storefronts floated past, and finally just ahead of them, with Johnny at last pumping the brake pedal, the church.

Then Danny's mother would invariably glance back at her children as if to say, "There, we did it this time, my little ones, we really got to church on Sunday."

Had she actually said so, or as much as murmured about his driving, or had she complained how dirty the trip made their faces, her husband might have slugged her and driven them straight home without so much as giving them a chance to genuflect. Upon such discretion swung the disjointed pendulum of Johnny Harp's moods.

One Sunday, his family got to church; another Sunday they stayed home, and Johnny might kick the bathroom door off its hinges.

Danny's father had come home from the war,

wounded and full of wild despair, an altered man who had seen comrades mowed down in the column ahead of him, leaving him standing alone not knowing why he was still alive, while their contorted bodies lay scattered over the bloody snow.

Another time, he had been shot out of a boat while crossing the Mosel and could not remember how he came to be upon the other side, half naked and shivering. The pictures of his children he carried with him were gone with his trousers and pack, and even now might be dissolving in the silt of some foreign backwater.

He had seen homeless urchins eating G.I. coffee grounds in the garbage heaps of Cologne.

So he forced into the mouths of his own children whatever they were slow to eat, and when they gagged and vomited between his fingers, he flung them to the floor in a swill of upended plates and stomachs.

He scattered his many war medals over the lawn around their house, he fired a souvenir Luger into the empty night sky, and he scared everyone.

It was said of the St. Barnaby town marshal that whenever Johnny's car hurtled by, whether twice the speed limit or faster, he would turn the nearest corner and pretend not to see. The town's stray dogs could look after themselves. Not for their sakes, nor even for the sake of any doddering fool who stepped off the curb would he challenge Johnny Harp. It wasn't from fear, he would insist, had anyone bothered to ask him why: *Johnny had been in the war, so leave him be.*

Lying in the grass one summer afternoon near a blooming peony bush, Danny gazed up into a pink globe with black ants toiling among its million petals drooping over him. Eyeing the glistening beads of nectar, he felt something hard in the small of his back. Danny twisted his hand under and then lifted into view an eagle with its talons gripping the swastika, the medal of victory in Europe.

Here was an insignia of his own misery perplexing him with the mixed emotions it caused.

People blamed the war for making his father the frightening man he was. They also called him a hero. Newspapers had recorded his valor in clippings that had not yet yellowed. Bunting draped storefronts for a small parade at his homecoming. The bells of St. Barnaby's rang nineteen times for all the months he had served and then twice more after a moment of silence for the times he had been wounded. Here in this medal was the alloy, the good and bad of it, fused and confused, bewildering him.

He knew he might love it if he tried hard enough. He knew he might hate it with less effort, for it deserved his hate. He might love or hate his father, and young as he was then, he couldn't predict finally how it would be. He rolled over and rising on one knee hurled the Medal of Victory out among the cornrows beyond their driveway.

Johnny Harp was away somewhere in his car, leaving his son to think what he would of him—to try or not to try, to love or to hate, the love which meant effort, the hate which meant simply not trying. But ultimately, he had thrown away the medal because he couldn't decide: he reacted from fear. Had the eagle slipped from his pocket and scuttled across the kitchen floor with his father standing by, or had his thoughtless piping on a toy whistle seemed to mimic the sound of artillery coming in, had anything whatsoever reminded his father of the war, his coiled rage would spring like a viper.

Danny and the other children hid behind their mother when that happened. Though she withstood his attacks, she shared their fright and built with them a private world away from him where none of them lived save when he was gone, and the fear withdrew like a peeping head in a rodent hole. Then the children frolicked around her. They were like the magic toys who dance when blinds are drawn over moonlit streets and the shopkeeper is away. When he returned, when his foot fell upon the doorsill, their whirling, gladsome madness stopped. Eyes shrank to painted slits on enameled wooden faces. Lips closing so suddenly on the breath of hubbub could not greet the returning man. His daughters could not kiss his cheek without death pallor on their own. He felt their lips trembling, saw his sons in the distance peering from around door frames, and swore that nobody on this spinning earth loved him.

During his frequent confinement for psychiatric treatment, these family respites were long enough and predictable enough to lose their neurotic verve. Danny spilled less of the water he carried into their kitchen from an iron pump in the yard. He tired of teasing his brother Jack. Jack tired of screaming his resentment. With Eileen and Mary, they played outside past the sunset of fair days and into the showers of cloudy ones until the usual games bored them, and they invented some of their own.

One of these began with each of them stationed alone on a side of their house. The object was to walk around it, again and again, without ever seeing or being seen by the others—past the peony bushes and the road to St. Barnaby on the east, beneath the single green ash tree on the south, on the west past clotheslines sagging across their view of an old poultry coop, then the row of cottonwoods on the north, around and around while remaining alone all the while, seeing no one and never being seen. If their pace went awry, as inevitably it did, with two of them trekking the same side at once, everyone lost. But if it had to end that way, the trick was to keep it going as long as possible, and then begin again.

They grew wonderfully adept at being in step out of sight of one another, and so, unconsciously, they made a prize of the solitude their lives never afforded them otherwise in the small house where they shared a bedroom of double iron beds, painted highboys, and divider drapes hung from a clothesline rope dividing brothers and sisters at opposite ends of the long, rectangular room.

Years would pass before Danny's memory of growing up would reduce itself to the single point that stood for himself alone. For a very long time these four points remained clustered, a constellation of him with his three siblings trailing him wherever he circled. He was seldom out of their sight, and the feeling that he was expected to look after them became so much a part of his thoughts that he never questioned it.

If he turned around and scowled his annoyance at being followed so much, they might hang back for a while within a doorway of the next room, or outside the other side of a shrub, west of the poultry coop when he was north in the windbreak, beyond a kink in the trail through a pasture woods across the St. Barnaby road, but as soon as he appeared nonchalant again, they caught up once more to tread on his heels and ask where he was going.

"Nowhere," he usually said, but they never believed it and kept right after him.

Early in life Danny had discovered a craving while hidden under his iron bed—a favorite place to escape from the others if he could get there without being seen—with its chenille coverlet pulled down till it touched the floor. Outside, perhaps, Eileen and Mary chased the hens again, happily screaming, happily forgetful of where he might be. Above him a coiling thicket of springs supported the mattress where he and Jack slept, and Jack now dozed. Through tiny rents, tufts of its wadding poked, and here a fact revealed itself winking through a fabric tear.

He didn't know enough about it to give it a name, but had anyone asked him about it later on, he would have said, "Solitude I discovered there and the peace that flowed into it."

It was peace of another sort they all found when the terrible Johnny was hospitalized and certain not to reappear without warning.

At such times their mother's family dared to visit. Uncles, aunts, and cousins Danny never saw otherwise gathered as if on tiptoe out of hiding to marvel at his absent father. So it seemed, at any rate, for they talked of little else, and they talked of Johnny Harp as a prodigy beyond belief.

They were deliberately vague whenever his children might overhear, deferential in the early days after the war with their prefaces like these: *"I grant you, the man went through a lot, but..."* and *"those who didn't fight shouldn't judge those who did, but..."*

Finally, though, the war's patriotic flush cooled and faded, and it became possible to criticize the dead Roosevelt and the living Mrs. Roosevelt; to question the stability of General Patton, likewise dead; to speak with renewed fondness of Lindbergh, though a pacifist; and to say of Johnny Harp without preface, *"All the good ones were shot dead over there—those that weren't worth a damn came home to raise hell."* This was the signal freeing the whole family to talk of him as they felt.

Pictures were taken after Sunday dinner with the sun yet high—inevitably the pictures—as though the Harp children might be swept away tomorrow and this would be the only record of their ever having lived. Uncle Emery strained to fit into his black box camera every conceivable combination: the little Harps alone, then with all their cousins, then girl Harps with girl cousins, then boy Harps with theirs, the reverse of this, and then the same with aunts and uncles and their mother—if she could be prodded into the camera's eye. Such possibilities seemed endless and endlessly appealing to Emery who wore them all out with it, pointing and shouting directions, snapping his shutter, so excited he'd be gasping toward the end, and if he hadn't run out of film and everyone's patience, he might have keeled over in a suffocating fit.

The adults returned to their coffee and beer and talk around the kitchen table, a remorselessly chanted communal mumble most of the time, for even if the children were out of earshot in the cornfields or the pasture woods, the prodigious Johnny, eighty miles away in a Veteran's hospital seemed likely to overhear and thunder his hatred of their backbiting.

And one such Sunday afternoon Danny came home from the pasture woods to see if his treasured pocketknife had been left behind in his room or lost in a rumpus with cousins among the trees.

Uncle Emery was speaking to his mother in a low, measured way giving his words the tone of a dare. "If I was you, Renee, I'd pack up these little ones and leave that worthless son of a bitch, war wounds or no war wounds, shellshock or whatever they call it."

Renee Harp sprang from her chair, "Daniel, what are you doing, sneaking in here?"

"I think I lost my knife." Danny squinted and twisted away from her accusing eyes. Uncle Emery was too bright to look at.

"Your knife," he sputtered. "Do you mean your jackknife?"

Danny nodded.

"Judas, what's that to make such a fuss about? I have right here the best three-blader you'll ever see, for love or money, and it's yours. Judas."

He drew it from a roomy pants pocket, and a

half dollar riding up with it spun around on the tabletop as he pulled Danny's hand from his eyes and tucked the knife into his fist.

"Emery, don't!" protested Renee, blushing for her brother, blushing for all of them. "You needn't do it, believe me—Daniel is old enough to know." She drew Danny to her till his cheek pressed against hers. He could feel her heart beating.

"Of course he's old enough, but it's my knife, and I want him to have it." Emery mussed the boy's hair, leaving a yellow hank of it hanging in his eyes, another yellow tuft in back standing up like a tail feather, and the odor of pipe tobacco on his face. He reached for his pipe, which lay beside an ash heap in a coffee saucer, and for the tobacco pouch in his shirt pocket.

Aunt Marge, Emery's wife, left her bottle of beer and pawed under the table for the vagrant half dollar.

"I got that baby in Mexico a year ago," bragged Emery through an ashy plume. "Its handle is real —Judas, someday I've got to show you all the pictures of our Mexico trip."

He didn't say what was real about the knife handle, but its insets were of black stone, and perhaps he thought them real obsidian. He took the half dollar from his wife and banged it flat upon the oil cloth, a pattern of tansies between yellow stripes with random circular cup stains.

"Heads or tails?" demanded Emery with his hand still over the half. "Heads or tails?"

"Heads or tails?" his mother coaxed.

"Tails," whispered Danny.

Heads it turned out to be, but Emery, undaunted, gave him the half anyway, and fishing further into his pockets, found another for Jack and quarters for the girls, all of which were likewise banged down upon the tabletop with the same false gusto.

Aunt Marge's beer bottle danced, and she leaped for it. The coffee saucer ashtray spilled its heap. Three, four gray plumes enveloped Emery's head. Then it was over.

"I guess these are yours," said Marge, handing Renee two hairpins she had found under the table.

Danny, released, went to his bedroom and laid his new pocketknife alongside the rusty old one forgotten upon his highboy. It was by far, as his uncle said, the best he had ever seen. So here again was the bewildering alloy of good and bad. Not having lost his own, he felt he was without claim to the one he was just given. Was keeping it dishonest then? Was it a bribe to begin with, and therefore a treason to his father? Did he love his father enough to return it?

Life advanced its array of unanswerable questions to dazzle him like myriad suns till he looked away. "All, Father," he had answered in the confessional without knowing well enough what he had admitted to begin with to say where it might have started or stopped.

So he learned to do what most people do—he guessed when he didn't know whether it was heads or tails, and he had to have an answer all the same. He guessed that Uncle Emery wouldn't accept his knife back, no matter what. He guessed that he shouldn't keep it anyway. He walked out across the St. Barnaby road into the pasture woods again.

The army of cousins had run far away to the other end where at the bottom of a hill the pasture became a sodden cow bog of moss-encased hummocks. He could hear their laughter and their high screams across this distance as coalesced and indistinguishable—brother from sister, cousin from cousin—as the various chipmunks and squirrels scolding him nearby with every step he took. He lowered his eyes and put his hands in his pockets.

There in the left he found his knife, and there

in the right he found the other—Emery's. He knew without looking, because it was longer than his, heavier, smooth and cold. Slowly he drew the knives out while raising his head to look up through the treetops where a squirrel stood still upon a branch and a white cloud drifted over the sun.

He held a knife in his left hand—his own, his treasure. Into his right hand went the other, and closing his eyes, without looking down, he spread his fingers and let both knives go.

In a pasture woodland trodden by cattle and horses with myriad paths and bi-ways as familiar as the furrows in his bare palms held skyward, he knew he could find his way back if he wanted. He also knew he would never come this way again. The squirrel raced away among branches as he ran beneath, down a path to join his cousins.

Come the snow of a winter after that, American Legionnaires tiptoed into the Harp kitchen with donations of Christmas gifts and food for a Veteran's family. They whispered greetings to mother and children, set down their parcels, and tiptoed away. Had anyone asked them why they whispered and tiptoed, they couldn't have said. Why were they so quiet and careful? Heroism wasn't forgotten—that had been what they meant to say, their message awkwardly delivered by men who could still tolerate toy whistles and the eating habits of their children, who drove the speed limit, and who left their snow tracks melting upon a linoleum floor where Johnny Harp's had long since vanished forever.

He had died alone in his car hurtling home from St. Barnaby to a supper table where a crock of beans had been set out to cool by his plate. Danny was fourteen. *Not forgotten,* the Legionnaires couldn't quite say, *were the families of those who escaped not dying to begin with and came home as good as dead because they no longer knew why they were alive.*

Uncles and aunts visited whenever they felt like it after that. None of them ever came out and said that Johnny's death left his family better off, but they believed it so, and they acted that way—though they still spoke in those same lowered voices in the farmhouse kitchen as if the eavesdropping madman might strike them dead from his grave between the church and the school.

A dozen years of pictures had been taken of the towhead Danny squinting, cringing, and scowling in the sun. Then Uncle Emery, who always drove like the spinster school teacher of used car salesmen's stories, died in an auto wreck of his own making. Danny was eighteen, grown so tall that the giant ragweed and early summer corn could no longer hide him.

He had learned to feel guilty before he learned to sin, learned to be afraid, learned about the alloy of good and bad, learned to guess when he had to, learned to look at things from an angle instead of straight on.

Some of this he owed to a grade-school nun and a kindly old priest, some to his mother and a fuddy-duddy uncle, but most of what he had learned he owed to his father.

He knew this, looking back on it all, looking back at the man who in distant memory still shone as bright as any god, too bright to behold straight on.

He strode back between the church and school and stared at his grave with the nation's flag fluttering alongside his marker and a bronze plaque declaring his heroism in defense of his country. *Even now* he couldn't quite figure out whether he hated this man or loved him more than he would ever love anyone.

Here, at the back of the cemetery a willow tree rooted near a board shed, and, because of its shadow and the barrier of its rock foundation, grew there in odd ways for a long, long time while new village graves crept closer to it. Then the shed where groundskeepers kept their implements collapsed beneath a weight of snow and was carted away in the springtime, plank and stone.

Robins scrutinized the spaces, ground squirrels burrowed and sunned themselves in the mounds they made among the encroaching cemetery mounds, daisies and sweet clover bloomed yellow and white, but the willow kept growing by its hundred old evasions, and if you hadn't known about the shed, you would wonder how it ever got to be that way with only wildflowers and hopping birds to avoid as it grew to embrace the sunlight.

And so, with his father and Uncle Emery forever gone from his life, carted away like a building torn down, stone and board, Danny stood alone there, growing to manhood and squinting in the shadows.

THE FAR END OF THE PARK

*I*n Cabin Twelve at the far end of the park Miss Thorpe would always be singing by herself, and the fall and winter I was fifteen, I walked up there late afternoons and listened beneath her window.

She sang old songs that I had never heard before, with names like *Stardust* and *Some Enchanted Evening*, songs you would never have heard anywhere else unless you had a grandma with a record collection.

After I listened a few times, I had many of them by heart, and it felt strange to be walking back home to Cabin Two with the sun going down and things like *The melody haunts my reverie, and I am once again with you* running through my head.

"Miss Thorpe up in Cabin Twelve is singing again," I would tell my mother.

"She's a singer," my mother said the first time she heard about it. "She was in a New York City musical once, but it was all downhill after that, I guess."

That year and the year after, I lived with my mother on the edge of a park where other people came for summer vacations and didn't come at all the rest of the year. This was called the *off season,* the weeks from Labor Day till June, when I was alone so much—except for school—that I began to think I was crazy for daydreaming and talking to myself and hanging around after a half-mile walk to hear Miss Thorpe sing. The off season days slowed down and lengthened. I learned what solitude was. I thought I had gone away inside myself and forgotten to send postcards home.

Cabins Three through Eleven were as empty as nine birdhouses in winter. They made you feel lonely the way empty buildings do. Just to walk by them all, spaced at hundred-yard intervals, was more of a trek than it was in the summer when the whole place was a clutter of laughter and shouts, cooking smoke, upended lawn chairs, and dogs lying in the shade by doorsteps and standing up to bark whenever the next stranger walked by. There might be a bicycle fallen over on its side right in the way of the park owner's three-reel lawnmower. He would have to hop off and pull it out of the way, then look at me as if he wondered why I hadn't done that for him.

Come Labor Day everything changed. With lawn chairs and fishing poles stuffed at crazy angles in their car trunks or tied to the tops of their SUV's, the tourists went away and, waving to me from their back seats were kids I had gotten to know and would never see again.

Only places that had once been noisy could seem as silent as the park after that. I couldn't hear five dogs barking whenever the moon came up. Cats weren't stalking the park chipmunks. The owner's lawnmower was stored in a utility shed with its side reels folded up, and it seemed to me much longer than the four months it was that Miss Thorpe was singing, I was walking afternoons between our cabin and hers, and my mother had said that it was all downhill after that.

The owner, a heavy set guy named Harmon, kept Cabin One for himself, but he spent the off season in Florida, leaving us as caretakers for half our rent.

Harmon came for supper the night before he left, and he told my mother that Miss Thorpe didn't have a job and might skip out without paying her rent.

"So keep an eye on her," he said.

He ate our meatloaf in big hunks cut with the side of his fork, all the while mopping up the drippings on his plate with a piece of bread he kept in his other hand. When he was finished, it looked as clean as plates that were still in our cupboard. He picked his teeth with his thumbnail and tilted his chair back from the table. He had a way with our furniture, I thought, that was meant to remind us that after all, he owned it as well as the room we sat in, as if we were his guests and he not ours, eating a meal my mom had cooked.

He told us about an alligator somebody caught in a Fort Meyers parking lot last winter.

"Don't you want to know how big it was?" he asked when I didn't bother to. "About sixteen foot," he said.

I knew he was lying, which is what I expected and why I hadn't asked him in the first place. He was sipping coffee now and eating a blueberry tart he dunked in the cup between bites. All the while he talked about things we should tend to while he was gone.

We were supposed to check the cabin doors and windows every day in case somebody broke in overnight, in which case we could notify the sheriff, which was better than waiting till he got back from Florida and discovered the crime weeks or months later.

"There's not a lot in these places that anyone would want to steal," he said glancing around at our furniture and then fixing his gaze on me, "but a few years ago a drifter broke into Cabin Six and must have lived there most of the winter. Made such a mess of the place that I couldn't rent it the following summer." He paused and seemed to be doing a mental calculation of how much that had cost him.

Since I hadn't asked him about the alligator, I thought I would make up for it by asking if they ever caught the drifter.

Harmon shook his head. "He broke the legs off all the chairs. For some reason, he sawed one of the beds in two, and the sheriff never caught up with him. Of course by the time I reported it, he could have been a thousand miles from here, which is where you come in." Again he looked at me.

I also "came in" whenever it snowed, since we were supposed to sweep as much of it from the cabin roofs as we could reach with a long-handled broom he left us. Otherwise the weight of it might warp the rafters, he said, and when it melted, water might back up and leak through the shingles.

Then he pushed himself away from the table, put on a yachtsman's cap he always wore and kept on his knee while he ate, and went home to Cabin One. When he opened the door, some yellow leaves blew in around his feet. When he closed it, they blew under our kitchen chairs.

"Fall's coming fast," my mother said, nudging the leaves into a little pile with her foot.

"Yes," I said, but it all seemed slow to me.

"I suppose most of what he wants us to do while he's gone, you can do after school or on weekends."

I nodded.

So after school, since I was supposed to be checking on things, including Miss Thorpe's whereabouts, I would walk along a dirt footpath through the park behind the cabins and then past the edge of a ravine to a hill where Cabin Twelve was all but hidden in the shade of oaks and maples three seasons of the year.

On the way back, I would take the narrow road running from Miss Thorpe's driveway past the front doors of the other cabins and out of the park to the highway. By the time I circled home, I had seen everything the owner expected us to check on.

Miss Thorpe had an old blue Buick she parked by her cabin door since only Cabin One had a garage. If I saw the Buick, I knew she was there, but all the same I would climb her hill for a closer look.

A few times I got there just as she was coming home or leaving, with her car lurching and weaving among the rocks and ruts in her driveway and her radio on loud enough that I could hear it even with her windows up. If she happened to see me out on the road, which once or twice she did, she would just wave and keep going as if she didn't think anything of it.

Her singing was just as carefree as that hand waving at me, effortless and clear, coming to me through the back wall of her cabin where I sometimes sat under a window by a gas tank before I started home. The window was always closed with a blue shade drawn over it. Even had Miss Thorpe looked out, she wouldn't have seen me on the other side of the tank with my knees drawn up under my chin.

Her songs seemed to ride out to me on the copper gas line, which gave her voice a metallic sound—a chill, vibrating hum that seemed to circle around my ears along the copper coiling over my head and then shoot down my spine at my shirt collar.

I might start out sitting in the grass with my shoulders propped against her cabin wall, but her singing made me slide, and soon I'd be stretched out full length on the ground with just my neck bent upright. *The days grow short when you reach September....*

Showery days I might have sung along, a season when the grass stays green much longer than it should and grows long enough that my mother began to wonder if we shouldn't try starting Harmon's lawnmower and mowing the whole park one last time.

Gray soggy days, I might have sung about the windless air that brings the leaves down in clear circles under their own trees, so that beneath every tree is one kind of leaf and one color.

Between rains, the sun dried everything, erased the circles, mixed up all the colors, the yellow and red which finally turned brown, curling at their edges, drifting around the corners of Miss Thorpe's cabin and into my lap.

Try to remember, try to remember the kind of September when grass was green and grain was yellow. Sun or rain, I was there.

Back home one afternoon, my mother showed me a postcard from Fort Myers. "Harmon says leave it be, the grass he means, so we shouldn't try mowing it. He says keep an eye on that Thorpe woman—she's two months behind with her rent."

"What's he think I'm doing?" was all I could say.

By mid November stronger winds had swept most of the leaves off Miss Thorpe's hill down into the ravine where, on my way, I could see them drifted into the brushy undergrowth. Night was coming sooner, the ground was colder, the sky would be darkening as I listened to her. She would be moving around as she sang, and her cabin floor creaked.

Sometimes I imagined her on a stage in a spot-lit circle—in the fashion of singers I had seen on television. She would sing to a make-believe bird on a bush, then to a policeman walking his beat with his nightstick swinging at his side, and then she would stroll to a park bench to finish her song.

As the weeks wore along, I got tired sooner and cold sooner, and she fell a third month behind with her rent.

Then there were days when I couldn't imagine anything, and I wondered what kind of a loony I might be to be spending so much time hunkered down by Miss Thorpe's cabin.

If I hadn't reached the top of her hill yet, even if I hadn't seen her Buick and wasn't sure her lights were on, wherever I was, I couldn't go further. When my thoughts ran off in that direction, I just turned back and ran after them, because I was always afraid I was going crazy from being alone so much. Didn't crazy people talk to themselves and imagine things that weren't there?

Other times I felt better about it. Late autumn has its warm days now and then. Sweet odors would drift out of the ravine and linger with me on Miss Thorpe's hilltop. I could have stayed up there forever, if she had sung forever, if I wouldn't have been missed for supper. Why is it that so much seems possible if only you wouldn't be missed for supper?

One November afternoon I spotted a flight of geese heading south and so high up, they were no more than a pencil slash in the sky over her cabin. Their screams mixing with her voice made me feel lonely and afraid, and for the first time I thought Miss Thorpe would skip out for sure, just what I was supposed to be watching for.

I heard more geese on my way home, but the sky was so dark I couldn't have seen them, and I didn't try very hard. I was walking past the other cabins, three with their backs to the ravine and the others out in the park along my footpath.

For some reason, I had reversed my normal routine and had walked up on the park road and then back home on the path instead. The cabins were dark and empty as they always were. Circling around each of them to check windows and doors, I started to doubt they had ever been otherwise, and to suspect that the owner's story about the drifter had just been another lie to go with his story about the alligator.

Behind me, I could see the light of Miss Thorpe's cabin. Ahead of me was the light of our own, while in between for the half mile was this darkness with the geese honking over it growing fainter and fainter and me stopping every hundred yards to twist a doorknob and tap a shutter fastener that was already hooked before I tapped it. It seemed to me that these two lights I walked between might be two ends of the same thing. Home might be on both ends of the park. Either way you went, there was something like duty or honor or love of your own kind at the end of it when the off season had swept everything else so clearly away.

When I got home, my mother asked if Miss Thorpe was still around.

"Yes," I said. "You can see her light up on the hill." It was one of those days that I hadn't gone all the way up there, so this was all I knew.

Then we went outside together and stood for a moment, looking at the light from Miss Thorpe's back window where a month ago I might have been sitting in the full light of the sun.

"Was she singing?" my mother asked. In the light from our own window I could see her breath, and I could tell from the way she spoke that she was shivering. "Harmon says that she's four months behind. When he gets back, he'll have the sheriff lock her out and keep her things till she pays. I hope it doesn't come to that."

"I didn't get close enough to hear her sing," I said.

Back inside I saw another postcard from Fort Myers lying picture up on the kitchen table, the same card he had sent the first time.

"Did you check all the cabins?" my mother asked.

I told her I did, and we ate supper.

That's how things went for another month, until the winter afternoon I saw Miss Thorpe leave.

Five minutes later, and I wouldn't have seen her go at all. I had come slowly down the park— on the road this time since the path behind was blocked with snow—sweeping snow from each cabin roof as I went and wondering if I was supposed to sweep Miss Thorpe's because Harmon hadn't said anything about that.

I enjoyed making it cascade off the eaves and its sifting sound when it mounded below, the kind of stuff crazy people would probably think was really important. So I took my time since if I was crazy, I thought, I might as well enjoy it. Before I finished with Cabin Eleven, the sky was black with the faintest stars you could ever see hanging in it.

That's when I saw Miss Thorpe's light go out above me on the hill. I heard a door slam, and by a light inside the Buick, I saw Miss Thorpe with what was a vase or a lamp and an armload of clothes she was putting in the back seat. I turned away and started running home, with the long-handled broom dragging behind me, bumping over the snow pack on the road.

I knew I wasn't running so I could report it. I had been all through this moment before it ever happened, and I knew when she really did leave, it would have to be this way.

I was running so I would hear less and see less and wouldn't have so much to lie about. Behind me I heard the Buick start up. I hopped off the road and hid behind a tree while she drove by heading out to the highway and leaving me for good.

As we ate supper that night, I waited for my mother to ask about her, but this night—like most of them recently—she didn't mention Miss Thorpe. I think she was tired of it, and never did want to spy on her.

"I got snow off the cabins," I said.

"Was there much of it?" she asked.

"A foot," I said, "but it comes off easy." I paused between my potatoes and a piece of fish, and waited for her to ask me. When she didn't, I knew I had to get it over with anyway. If I had to think about lying to her, I'd never do it, so I said straight out that Miss Thorpe was singing fine as usual, and for good measure since it was the season, I said she sang some Christmas songs.

"I wish I could have heard them," my mother said.

It pained me that I had gone that far in fooling her, but at least she wouldn't have to either turn Miss Thorpe over to the sheriff or lie to the owner. She could talk about snow on the cabin roofs and Christmas plans for us. She was free of it. It was the end of Miss Thorpe, and with this much behind me, I knew I could keep it going till she was as far enough away as that drifter Harmon lied to us about. He would never catch up with either of them and make them pay.

It worried me that her cabin light was out. After two days of thinking about it, I went up there and let myself in since she hadn't locked it. In a shaft of moonlight over my shoulder, I could see her brass key lying on the kitchen table.

Her table was exactly like ours, except that it was brown —as far as I could tell with my shadow falling across it—and ours was yellow. I couldn't see much else in there without stepping beyond the doorway.

There was an old stuffed sofa like ours and a couple of chairs like our chairs. She hadn't broken their legs off. I was sure she hadn't sawed a bed in two. That had never happened anyway.

Since all the cabins were alike, Miss Thorpe's

light switch would be where ours was. Without having to look, I reached for it along the wall. After I flicked it on, I shut the door and turned away, also without looking, because I had seen enough and didn't want to see more of her cabin than the moonlight had already shown me. Even though she was gone for sure, I felt like it was her place still, and I had no business being there.

Harmon returned a few weeks before the off season ended. Right away he found out that Miss Thorpe was gone. He tried blaming my mother. He called the sheriff, but nothing more came of it as far as I could tell.

"We could see her light on every night," she told him, and that was the truth.

When he stormed back to his cabin, she said to me, "You said you could hear her singing, but he says she's been gone for months."

"I thought I could hear her," I said fending off the reproach in her voice.

A few weeks from now, the other cabins would be full again. Dogs would be barking at strangers strolling by, and cats would be after the chipmunks. Time was already moving faster. Days that were longer in light seemed to be shortening otherwise.

I knew I could make it to another summer,

just as every once in a while after Miss Thorpe left, I climbed her hill and hung around her cabin, pretending she was still there. I knew I would be all right.

Sometimes to see more, I had learned, you needed less light. You needed less noise and clutter. The wind had to sweep away everything you might have thought mattered. What remained you could count on.

It was the same on both ends of the park. Coming through the darkness either way, you could find it. I knew I wasn't crazy, even if I thought I could hear her singing long after she was gone, so I said to my mother one last time, "I thought I could hear her," and that also was the truth.

BILLY STILLWATER

*H*e looked like what you expected an Indian to look like, if you got your ideas about his sort from watching dated Westerns. He had a face like the one you might see in comic books. The first time you saw him, he looked so familiar you thought you met long ago, and perhaps for that reason, summer tourists passing through the Reservation on a shortcut to Canada would pick him out to ask directions, if he happened to be there, on the edge of a road at an intersection, as they approached.

Once, with perfect seriousness and without the least suggestion of mocking him, one such even lowered a window, raised a hand, and said, "How!"

"I don't know how," Billy replied with a grin and a shrug.

Another time, they asked to take his picture, and he agreed, despite a dated suspicion that each photograph taken took something away, leaving a little bit less of what was there to begin with.

Billy had already lost enough for other reasons to make it seem like not much of a gamble. So three kids scrambled out of a van and stood two on one side of him and one on the other. The smallest of them, a little girl, even took his hand. Afterwards, they thanked him and showed him the picture in their digital camera, and the man who had taken it offered him five dollars. Who would have thought he would refuse?

Billy didn't accept handouts. And so the spell was broken. Billy became a stranger to them, and the stereotype became roadkill.

Summers spawned such stories. Winters brought other offerings.

Whatever Billy Stillwater might have thought of as his family had either moved away somewhere or been dead for so long that already twenty years ago when he was twenty-six, it seemed to him he'd been alone most of his life.

And so, it wasn't that much of a change for him when he moved into an abandoned shack a day or so before the woman he thought would be living there with him left the Reservation and never came back.

He didn't go there to live alone—he could have stayed where he was and done that—but when she didn't show up, and then he figured out she wasn't coming at all, he stayed there by himself because he didn't know what else to do. Regardless, what would have been the point to alternatives promising no more of something he already didn't have?

"I had a plan A," he used to say, enjoying the wryness of using white man's lingo he'd picked up somewhere, "but I didn't have a plan B." He shrugged, and his grin revealed more missing teeth than teeth. With time, whenever he talked about his abandonment, he managed to seem even more amused, as if he had lost in a game of hide-and-seek, and the right thing to do was be a good loser.

He never heard from his woman again.

He was a good loser.

Now he was a forty-six-year-old Indian man, an old one at that, because all those years of living off woods and lakes—whatever they yielded—of hunting deer and netting fish and getting them sometimes and starving when he didn't, of sleeping half frozen on one side and half cooked on the side nearest his barrel stove, of cutting firewood in snow up to his chest when his yard pile didn't get him through the coldest winters, of being eaten by wood ticks in the spring and deer flies in the summer—all such things together—in a life as raw and lonely as the wind whistling around his shack on a January night, dried him up, broke him down like hard frost on a plant, and made him look like everybody's idea of an Indian, with wrinkles and color in all the right places.

Today he had a letter folded into the left pocket of his wool plaid shirt. It had been there since early this afternoon when he found it in his box at the Reservation store. Because he never expected anything to show up there, or anywhere else for that matter, and because he couldn't read regardless and had no expectations, he had no habit of checking his mail.

It took a stray thought, which might come once a week or every other week, most likely to appear with prompting when he needed a pack of cigarettes and Isabel Fisher, who ran the store would say, "Billy, it's time you clean out your mail box." And this time she added, "And don't just throw everything away without looking at it because for once you got a letter."

So, instead of pulling out the wad of shopping flyers from Sawhill stores and throwing the lot away with a sweep of his arm toward a trash can, he poked around till he found the letter, and then threw everything else away without looking at it.

"How long?" he asked Isabel, stuffing it into his shirt pocket before she could answer. She stood in the post office section of her store under a sign, a piece of tin hanging from the ceiling by two wires with the words *Post Office* upon it in black, block print letters.

"If you mean *how long* a letter is it, Billy Stillwater, I couldn't tell you because I don't snoop in people's mail," said Isabel. "If you mean *how long* it's been there, then I can tell you since yesterday morning—do you want me to read it for you?"

Billy shook his head, thinking that if Isabel Fisher read his letter, she would share it with half the Reservation coming to her store every week for their mail and groceries.

He took it from his pocket where a corner peeked above the edge, folded it in two, and put it back again, this time concealing it completely, while Isabel's small, dark eyes squinted as if fixed on a fine detail now hidden there. She stepped out from under her post office sign and into the grocery part of her store where another sign hanging from the ceiling said *goods*, this one in a hand scrawl of black enamel over white, neither paint hiding the red it used to be and the words *Coca-Cola*.

"Do you want anything then, Billy Stillwater?" Isabel asked. She was standing in front of a shelf of canned soup looking at him as if she wanted to read his letter more than anything *he* could have wanted, and she was trying to recall the magic words that would get it back out of his shirt pocket.

"Not today, Isabel," he said. "There's only one of me, you know, and I don't want nothing."

"You're lucky, Billy Stillwater, if that's the case. There's some around here that is more than one and wants a lot, but they don't have nothing just the same."

He nodded and turned his back on her and the rows of soup cans behind her, the barrel stove nearby with heat pouring out of it, and the ragged pieces of oak bark on the linoleum floor just in front of it from the logs she had thrown in since she swept this morning.

"You know you can't read it," she said as he opened the door.

A cold draft pushed by him and swirled around Isabel's legs.

"Maybe I can," he said stepping out into the street. The door banging shut behind him cut short the sound of her laughter. Only then did he think he'd forgotten to buy his cigarettes. He shrugged and kept going across the street just the same.

On the other side where he'd parked his old Chevy was the Bureau of Indian Affairs hospital, strangely built so that its brown brick backside faced the street while its front looked out upon a vacant wooded lot. Like so much else on the Reservation, it seemed half-conceived.

The snow hitting his face out there was not so much falling as spinning down in big, dry flakes from broken clouds like gray wooly fog rolling over the Reservation treetops. Who would have thought that anything so fragile could bite the skin? It was one of those squalls that come some January days when the wind is northwest, the cold too heavy to breathe in deeply, and the sky not clear enough to let sun through even half the time.

He knew somebody in the hospital who would read his letter for him and not tell anybody else what was in it, and that was important to a man who had lived so privately that he couldn't live any other way, who, because he couldn't read, thought everything written a mystery. That Nellie Kennedy would read his letter and keep it to herself was one of the few certainties the old BIA building held for him, even though it had been there since he was a little boy, and he had even lived in it after a fashion for a month about five years ago when he was recovering from pneumonia, or almost dying of it, until Nellie came to his bedside.

He had been struck down at the very beginning of the wild rice harvesting season. He had gone out the first day only, and the rest he had spent in the hospital. He remembered paddling upstream on the river toward its outlet on the big lake where most of the wild rice grew in broad shallows of the southern shore. But he never got that far before he let go of his oars and drifted back in the current because he was too weak to paddle or even guide with a pole his homemade boat.

He might have drifted downstream until he ran aground somewhere and died had he not been spotted collapsed over the gunwale by

others who were then making their way upstream for the harvest. They snared his boat and
brought him half conscious to the hospital. There
he had stayed for the next four weeks while the
shallows surrendered its rice to other hands, and
he was surrendered to Eleanor Kennedy's.

A white nurse who worked in the Public
Health Hospital, she had been on the Reservation
about as long as he had been living alone on the
river narrows. She might have been ten years
older than Billy, but anyone looking at them together would have mistaken it the other way.

White workers by the score wandered on and
off the Reservation every year, all of them with
skills the Indians needed or the government
thought they needed. As soon as they found other
work, most of them got out and tried to forget
they had ever been there.

Among those who stayed, many led lives of
desperate waiting, hoping each year the next
would set them free, serving their time as if in a
penitentiary for whatever crime drove them from
their own society in the first place. For some of
them this proved to be a life sentence.

A very few others stayed for life because they
found their niche on the Reservation, saw they
were needed there, and would have thought it a

crime instead to turn their back on it. This was Eleanor Kennedy whose niche was paying close attention to people who were used to being ignored, Reservation people who were sick, lonely, and invisible.

She must have begun reading to Billy before he was well enough to know it. Even before he could open his eyes and know night from day, there was her soft chant, at first a mere hum in his imagination. It could have been something spinning in a corner of the next room. Then he opened his eyes and found her sitting on a folding chair near his bed. She read to him from magazines and the comic strips of the *Minneapolis Sunday Tribune*. She pointed out each colored square, then told him what was happening in it. She read poems from a collection of poetry she carried around like a prayer book:

> *Who would have thought my shrivel'd*
>   *heart*
> *Could have recover'd greenessee? It*
>   *was gone*
> *Quite underground; as flowers depart*
> *To see their mother-root when they are*
>   *blown;*
> *Where they together*

All the hard weather,
Dead to the world, keep house
  unknown.

He didn't have to ask. "It's about being young again, Billy, it's about coming back when you thought you would never make it."

He dropped his head onto the pillow from which he had raised himself on one arm. He dreamt of roots and flowers, of gales, snow-storms, and *Beetle Bailey*. Gradually he was well enough to go home. Ever since, when he needed to have something read, he turned to Nellie.

But this time he got back into his car, which was in front of a hospital service entrance, and raced an engine whose idling had turned to the ominous chug and rattle of approaching death. He had left it running to keep his windshield clear of ice, and because, in weather like this, with a car this old, it took an act of faith to turn it off and think it would start again.

A feeble current of warm air blew out of the heater. It wasn't enough to warm his legs, but it was enough to feel better than the cold that was everywhere else.

He thought his letter might be from the government because in place of a stamp it had an eagle printed. He tore it open across that end and unfolded the single white sheet he found inside. Government paper always felt more important than any other. It felt like money, and this letter had that feeling as he studied its rows of black type leading to a blue signature at the bottom.

He always thought if he looked hard enough at writing he would be able to make some sense of it. Most other things he knew were like that: tracks in the snow, clouds over the treetops thickening toward the west. If you looked, you could tell where things came from and where they would go. You could see what you had missed overnight while you slept, and now what lay ahead at daybreak.

But writing wasn't like that. It was like something hiding from him. It should have yielded to his scrutiny if only he could outlast it, but somehow it always outlasted him. Nellie Kennedy would have to help.

He glanced at his gas gauge and turned the ignition key to save the little he had left in the tank. From his key chain a rabbit's foot dangled. It had come with the key and the car when he bought it for a hundred dollars of his wild rice money last fall. It was a dirty rabbit's foot, grey and greasy to touch, as if a hundred hands had been trying to get their luck out of it and not getting much. The engine rattled to a halt, then clattered back to life for a second, before stopping dead. The trickle of heat curling up around his feet became instantly a rising layer of cold.

He got out and shuffled to the hospital entrance, pushing one foot in front of him, then the other, the way children sometimes go over a slippery surface. His tracks looked like those of a skier. The letter was back in his shirt pocket along with the rabbit's foot and key. He opened his mouth to take a deeper breath before he stepped inside, and felt for a second a snowflake melting on his tongue.

"What do you want?" a young Indian woman at a reception desk asked him. With her question came a tone and a look in her eyes suggesting he had no right to want anything from her.

"I don't need nothing," said Billy for the second time that hour.

The eyes looking straight back at him said *nothing* was just what he would get.

"Where's Nellie?" he asked.

"Where she is every afternoon—if you need nothing, what do you want her for? You don't look sick to me, Billy Stillwater."

Billy shrugged, fingering the letter in his shirt

pocket, and shook his head without saying more. He knew all about these young Indians who went to school off the Reservation somewhere, came back, and worked for the government. They didn't respect his sort, and he had nothing to say to them.

On a table beside her desk, a phone rang. When she turned away to answer it, he dodged down a long hallway, past rows of office doors, every one like the last he passed, except that some were open and most were closed. Behind one of the closed ones, he heard the rattling of an old typewriter, behind another some women giggling and voices he recognized.

When he reached the end, a glass door and then a sliding fire door led into the Public Health Service Wing and the Indian hospital. This wasn't the regular way into the hospital, but if he had come in from the other side of the building at the main entrance, he would have found more desks and more sets of eyes even harder to slip past. Moreover, Nellie worked near this end.

He found her beyond the fire door in a small waiting room where the only other person was a boy seated on a stool with his mouth open and his tongue sticking out while she pointed a light in and attempted to peer inside. The hallway, the room itself, had that sweet antiseptic odor he would never forget from his days in the hospital when he was there long enough to lose track of it till he missed it the minute he was outside again. The boy, he thought, might be one of Bernard Singlefeather's. Nellie switched off her little flashlight and dropped it into an apron pocket. Billy stood in the doorway with the letter unfolded in his hand.

"I'll be with you in a second," she said glancing his way. "You don't need to see the doctor," she said to the boy. "You need a dentist. You've got a bad tooth in there—that's your problem." She took a small notepad from her other apron pocket, wrote a few words on it, folded it in half and handed it to him. "When we're done here, take this back to the desk up front and tell them you need to see a dentist Now I have to check your temperature. —And how are you getting along these days, Billy?" she asked over her shoulder.

The boy, now with a thermometer in his mouth, having twisted around to get a better look at Billy, was staring cross-eyed over the glass tube at his letter.

Billy said he was the same as always and shrugged, which was a habit of his. "But I got to know what this is—it's from the government, ain't it?"

Nellie laughed as she took his letter and unfolded it. "Lord, don't tell me they've drafted you." She laughed again, put on her glasses, and began to read. "Take the load off your feet, Billy," she said, pointing to a chair opposite the boy.

"I'm too old for the army," Billy said. "What would they want with an old Indian?" He started to think vaguely about the war as he sat down. Nothing he could think of was quite that vague and far away.

The boy tried to say something with the thermometer in his mouth yet.

"Hush, don't talk," Nellie said. She didn't look up from the letter, but spoke into it, as if talking to it and not the boy. It was the letter she wanted to quit saying things.

"I didn't ask you," said Billy. "I was asking Nellie Kennedy here." He well remembered a time when no Indian boy on the Reservation would have said a word in a conversation where he wasn't invited.

"You one of Bernard Singlefeather's boys?" he asked. When the boy didn't answer but instead lowered his eyes and stared at the floor, Billy knew he was a Singlefeather.

Nellie glanced up from the letter and pulled the thermometer from his mouth with a quick, nervous movement that had the appearance of anger.

A door slammed out in the hall, and the young woman from the desk appeared in the doorway. "He just comes sneaking down here behind my back," she said glaring at Billy, but speaking to Nellie. "Nobody, except people who work here, is supposed to go into the hospital this way, so he thinks he can."

"Never mind, Belinda," said Nellie. "Billy just forgot."

"Well, he shouldn't forget he don't work here."

"Never mind," Nellie said again, and then she turned to the boy once more. "Now you have a fever." The boy didn't move or look up from the floor. "So you'll have to wait for the doctor to have a look at you, then we'll send you to the dentist." She pointed to a row of chairs across the room from Billy. "Sit over there till the doctor gets here."

"He sneaked behind my back," Belinda repeated, this time raising her voice to make her accusation sound more important than Nellie seemed to think it was.

"Do you feel okay enough to sit up, or do you

want to lie down somewhere?" she asked the boy. He replied by shuffling across the room and sitting in a chair beside a window.

Belinda spun back out into the hall, the sounds of her heels on the wooden floor lasting until the glass door eased shut behind her.

"She could have saved herself the trouble," Billy said more to himself than to Nellie who seemed to be reading his letter from the beginning again. Meanwhile the Singlefeather boy began leafing through a magazine, leaving Billy to ponder with some amazement that *he* could read. He studied the low sky beyond the window at the boy's elbow. Out there were things he could read, things that did not hide from him.

It had become a cloudless, dark blue sky now, blue as raw steel. The wind had swept every cloud from view, and he knew from that and the sky color that the sun was going down. A brutally cold night lay ahead.

The window looked out upon a vacant lot stretching the entire length of the hospital wing on that side. It was a place most patients could see from their beds, and anywhere else it might have been landscaped like a park and planted with trees. But on the Reservation it was a wasteland of ragged clumps of cinquefoils scattered among tufts of crabgrass in the summer, and in the winter a snowfield, featureless save for the random dry stem and circles of dog tracks that came and went as the drifting snow erased them. Over all this emptiness, the sharply slanted sunlight cast a faint glow.

He turned to Nellie who had removed her glasses and was staring at him. The letter lay open in her lap.

"What does it say?" he asked.

She leaned toward him. "I never knew you had a son," she whispered.

"I don't," he said, not whispering, but loud enough for the boy to hear if he wanted to eavesdrop. Nellie had a habit of joking with him, and he was always prepared to enjoy it.

"You never had a son?" she asked, not really like a question but like something she was trying to understand. It wasn't a joke.

"I ain't never had a woman—Nellie, you know that." Now that he could see she wasn't teasing him, he lowered his voice to hers.

"I've heard people say that," she said as her eyes lowered to the letter whose paper seemed metallic blue lying upon her white uniform. She read one word to him.

"Sharon?" she said.

It all opened up for Billy Stillwater. The name was a key, and it fit in a door belonging to a part of his life now so far away that he might never have gone back there in his thoughts again, except for hearing Nellie say it in the heavy silence of this room where the three of them sat waiting.

The Singlefeather boy had slid the magazine onto a chair beside him. His head was down, and his dark hair dangled over his forehead and eyes as he seemed to study the toes of his shoes. Billy knew that any son of his would have to be older than this boy, much older, alive as long as the years he had been living on the river narrows. At the same time, any son of his seemed much younger, really just a new baby coming into this world.

His mother would be Sharon who was crying the last time he saw her, and though he couldn't get her to say why, he thought he knew why, and so he said to her, "It'll be all right. We'll go out there, and we'll be all right."

Her voice didn't sound the way he knew it, and her eyes had the metallic glitter of stars on a midwinter's night. He studied those two stars searching for some sign that she understood him.

"You hear me," he kept saying, sometimes like a question and sometimes as if telling her she must hear him now, but either way he said it, he never knew what she heard between her sobs and broken, high-pitched ranting through teeth nearly clenched. He could still feel her tight little fists thrust against his stomach, still hear her words, as if first swallowed and then chewed, then spit out, about her white father who hated him because his daughter was only sixteen and half Indian, and Billy Stillwater was twenty-six, too old for her, and too Indian to have her whatever his age.

Had she heard what Billy said? Not knowing, he waited half the next night in a borrowed car parked a quarter mile down the road from her house, out of sight beyond a bend there. Would she go away with him? He had already claimed an abandoned shack out along the river narrows where others before them—some having grandchildren by this time—had gone when there was nowhere else to go.

The night wore on with Billy walking from his car to a point on the road bend where her house could be seen, its lights going out one by one on his successive surveys till at last all its windows were blackened. Stars paraded overhead, the constellations of the waning season exchanging places with the next, and still no sign of her. He thought she might be locked in and couldn't leave, or perhaps she hadn't understood his plan in the first place. How could he know? He would see her tomorrow, and they would try it all over again. With the sun rising, he drove back into the village. He never did meet her tomorrow or ever after that, and there was no way of trying anything again. He had plan A, but no plan B.

In a few hours, he would learn they had moved out, loading everything into a truck that had come on the Reservation at sunrise, which in fact he met as he drove the other way. The whole family had gone, without as much as leaving word at the post office for their mail to follow. It was the way life began and ended on the Reservation: coming and going in the night, disappearing without a word, reappearing without explanation. It was a river flowing in both directions. But even so, Billy couldn't believe it this time.

He walked into her father's yard and shouted for her to come out of a house so empty that he might himself have moved into it. He peered in at each window whose distant light he had studied so vainly the night before. Curtains no longer blocked his view, and he could search rooms as vacant as his own life seemed suddenly to become. He turned away and walked back out to the road. A quarter mile away he passed the tire tracks of his borrowed car still imprinted in sand along its edge. He met his own footsteps.

Now he was saying to Nellie that he once knew a girl who had moved away, saying it to her as a matter of fact without any of the emotion he had felt then.

"Maybe I understand, if that's the case," Nellie said, "but I wished I didn't." She got up and walked over to the window, black enough out there now to turn it into a mirror so that she could see herself there, the boy at her elbow, and Billy seated behind her waiting. Then motioning for the boy to follow, she crossed the room to the hallway door. "I think we'll send you running along first to the dentist," she said, "and when he's done with you, he can send you back here if he thinks you should see the doctor—give me that note I wrote for you." She added instructions to that effect, and sent him on his way. Stepping back inside, she closed the door behind her.

"If only I couldn't make any sense of it," she said to Billy. "If I couldn't read either, or if it were just another mistake the government made, I could tell you it's nothing, and you'd go away, and maybe that's the way it ought to be." She knelt on the floor by his side and took his wrist in her hand.

"From what it says here, you and this Sharon had a son —you never knew that?"

"Never," he answered with a tremor in his voice.

"Never," she whispered.

"I thought maybe she could be having a baby," he said. "I pretty well figured that had to be it, but she went away, and there wasn't any more to it."

"You never heard from her or her family."

He shook his head.

The hand on his wrist tightened. Nellie's eyes glistened.

"There was more to it, Billy, I'm afraid, though why you never heard about it I couldn't say. I've been here on the Rez so many years, and told so many fathers about their sons. Sometimes it's been happy, and sometimes sad. I've gotten used to it being either way, but this isn't the same. It says here you had a son, you and this Sharon, and they couldn't find any other way of telling you about it, but he's been killed—oh, Billy, I hate to say it—he's been killed in the war just last week...."

Outside a half hour later, after Nellie had

walked him past Belinda's desk to the employee entrance door, Billy was sitting again in his old Chevy. Across the street, Isabel Fisher had just turned out the lights and locked up the post office store. In front of him, lights were going out in office parts of the old BIA building and coming on in the hospital wing. People were filing out, getting into their cars, and driving away without warming them up. One of them was Belinda who had hissed at him on the way out.

Clouds of car exhaust filled the street. Billy's car hadn't run long enough, so he waited for that thin current of warm air coming up from its heater, telling him he could safely move it without killing the engine.

He had been sitting there trying to think about his girl again, mostly just struggling to picture her face. He couldn't get it back—she was too far away, and she was too dead. Nellie read it from the letter. "*Son of Sharon Saunders, _deceased_, and William Stillwater.*" Her name hadn't been Saunders when he knew her, and no one in this world had ever called him William. It might have been the first time he had ever heard it.

He tried thinking of himself as William, but it seemed to be somebody else. It was almost the strangest thing about it. How could he be William who had a son he never heard of until he heard he was dead, stillborn that way in the war someplace, coming into this world and passing out of it almost in the same breath? How could he be William, and how could Sharon be dead?

He felt a warm rivulet circling his ankles, eased his car out onto the street, and drove away, still without the cigarettes he'd come for.

*BILLY STILLWATER WITH 'UNCLE SAM' Bird at his side will eventually visit the Fort Snelling grave of the highly-decorated soldier son he never knew.

THE LONG WAY AROUND

*B*arnaby sat in his car in the grip of old habits. He was immediately across the street from Lance's apartment. From there, he would walk about a half mile to Lance's radio station on the second floor over a bakery. At the end of it, they could walk back together with perhaps the light snow still falling. Snow lent a nice touch with Christmas near, and in days past, he'd sought nice touches and had some of his best talks with Lance while walking. Somehow, not having to look at each other had made things easier.

At least Lance knew he was coming—if he'd gotten his postcard from London. Regardless,

Barnaby knew where to find his son. He'd heard Lance on his car radio a minute before with twenty minutes to go on his Saturday morning air shift, time enough to walk there.

It hadn't always been this way. In Lance's adolescence, visiting him had become a game of hide-and-seek around town with Barnaby on the trail, punching doorbells, prowling the shopping mall, and circling through video game arcades and whatever else passed for a teen hangout. These possibilities were sufficiently limited that he usually found Lance in time to sip a coke with him, eat a burger, and ask a few questions, but occasionally Barnaby drove home empty-handed.

When he finally caught up with Lance on his next visit, the boy would be apologetic and perplexed. He wouldn't fail to say he was sorry, but at the same time, his eyes seemed to ask, *Why are we doing this, Dad?*

Barnaby, himself never far from the same question, feared the answer enough to be glad Lance never asked. Those weekend trips on the road to visit him had provided time enough to come up with the truth, except of course the truth was the last thing he wanted to know. So Barnaby avoided it. Instead, he kept watch for deer in the ditches autumn and spring, fireflies summers, and patches of ice on the road ahead in any season not summer.

The truth seemed to be all his efforts to stay close to his son were an accumulating failure, an ever-increasing number rolling up on some pitiless odometer of the spirit, and still he couldn't stop doing it.

If visitation was about keeping a normal relationship with one's child, for this dad it felt like a hopeless effort to cradle liquid in cupped hands. As Lance grew older, normalcy slipped through the cracks and drained away just at the point Barnaby thought he might taste it.

The sheer effort to keep things normal turned everything abnormal. If you live in the same house with your kid, you might not leave your beer and your lawn chair on the patio to walk upstairs to ask if he enjoyed the matinee that afternoon. But if you and your kid live in separate houses a hundred miles apart, you don't think twice about driving two hours each way and spending a hundred dollars on gas and food to ask, not about the matinee—because you wouldn't have known about that—but to ask the sort of banal, rehearsed, and repeated questions that people leading separate lives rely upon for icebreakers.

How was school? Anything exciting happen lately? Any news? How's the rabbit?

Barnaby learned to despise all such questions, just as he despised the trite messages of appreciation he received from creditors he paid on time and the birthday cards his bank and insurance agent sent him without fail.

The first day Barnaby and Lance lived in separate homes was the day Lance began to drift away. Drifting, in fact, only described the early days of their separation, when the widening gap might not be noticed until a year went by. You knew some drift had occurred when a sense of strangeness crept in. Lance would mention that he'd forgotten to feed his rabbit. Barnaby would say, "I didn't know you had a rabbit—when did you get a rabbit?"

The rabbit, nosing about in a pen built by his mother's new boyfriend, had been hopping out of sight on the fringes of their last three visits. It finally popped up looking for food. Then there was the boyfriend, somebody named Guy who would have gone through several packs of razors and at least two large tubes of toothpaste before

Barnaby knew that he and Lance were sharing a bathroom.

It took Barnaby's mother, who lived in the same town, to break this news. "I hadn't wanted to ask before this, but you know how Lance likes to chat me up from time to time. Lately, I'm hearing a lot about this Guy?"

There followed a spell of confusion about whether they were talking about a guy or a guy named Guy. Either way, since he couldn't admit having heard nothing and not even knowing about Guy, Barnaby appeared amused that the guy was Guy, a good joke as far as it went.

He acted unsurprised and said, "Lance doesn't have anything to say about the guy." That wasn't a joke and the truth only as far as it went.

So here they were almost from the first, he and Lance, losing track, overlooking details, and keeping secrets, both of them unprepared and on their guard, in a new world of rabbits and live-in boy friends with carpentry skills. Later on it would be Lance's girlfriends and keg parties in gravel pits Barnaby might only discover in chance revelations between bites of a hamburger and pulls on a coke straw. What had begun as drifting away had become the acceleration of a kid in a juiced-up pickup with a young lady to impress. Though Barnaby raced to keep up, Lance pulled away. Barnaby had become a dog chasing cars.

And like a dog with this habit, he couldn't quit. He couldn't even slow down and do it less often.

Ten years passed this way, a decade of birthday presents over pizza slices with wads of gift wrap at their elbows tumbling onto floors; a decade of trying to think of things to say, of losing track or never knowing or hearing about it afterwards; a decade on the road for Christmas Eve, when visitation fathers hit the road alongside carloads of families off to see grandparents. Single men at neighboring gas pumps exchanged the knowing glances of fellow travelers with gifts in backseats, trunks, and pickup boxes. These were the new Santa Clauses in an age of broken marriages, hopelessly trying to keep up.

North every weekend drove Barnaby, first with musical tops and farm sets, with a tricycle and then a bicycle, with a fielder's mitt, a fishing rod, a snow dish, then a sled, then cross-country skis, a CD player, a 35mm camera, and even a razor when he noticed Lance had begun shaving. Most of this disappeared into Lance's life and was never seen by Barnaby again. He might have been sending things to a children's mission in a third world country.

He fought despair with strategies. "Bring your mitt along next weekend, and we'll go somewhere and practice catching." A time or two he saw the mitt.

He took Lance fishing. "That's not the rod I gave you, is it?"

"That one broke," said Lance.

Lance pulled farther and farther away. Guy had given him one of *his* rods, much the better than Barnaby's gift.

The following week, on his next trip north, Barnaby brought a better rod yet, and learned in the ensuing talk about fishing that Lance and Guy had been out in Guy's boat only the day before. How were they supposed to fish from shore when Lance had been out in Guy's boat? Guy, on the inside, never having to figure out anything, seemed to have all the advantages.

Barnaby gave up fishing, bought Lance a violin, and arranged for lessons from a local music student. He wouldn't have been surprised to learn that Guy played cello or fiddled in a bluegrass band. It came to worse instead.

Perhaps, given his twisted purpose, it was fitting that this implement, meant to assault Guy's brain during Lance's home practice, should turn against Barnaby himself and become a symbol of his hopeless effort. Lance both hated the violin and hated quitting for fear of what his dad might think. Barnaby quit asking questions. The violin, though not even a full-sized one, became a room to walk by on tiptoe without either of them daring to glance through a door half-opened.

Then he met Guy—it seemed almost by accident—in the bank lobby on a Monday morning with a personal check in his hand needing approval. Right there, a hundred miles from home in front of Barnaby's desk, stood the mythic Guy, not even as tall as Barnaby, who himself wasn't very tall. Guy didn't seem to know who he was, or maybe he was simply saying he didn't even care. Barnaby, in a mood to play the same game, approved the check with barely a glance at his ID, turned briskly away, and picked up his phone.

From that day forward, Barnaby owed a lot to Guy.

After work, standing on his garage rooftop with wood scraps left over from a repair project, Barnaby thought of Guy's nonchalance in accepting things as they were. What was there about standing at an unaccustomed elevation

looking at customary things to make philoso-
phers of us all?

He threw three boards one by one from the
gable end and watched them land one by one all
with their nails sticking up, their positions deter-
mined either by bad luck or the laws of physics.
He knew about bad luck, but he didn't know
enough about physics to say for sure whether
boards with nails protruding, like falling cats, will
always come to earth a certain way. Perhaps
trouble being more noticeable and much of the
time more memorable, there only *seemed* to be
more of it.

Who noticed a board that had landed with its
nails pointing down buried harmlessly in the
earth, innocuous as wisdom teeth that never cut
the gum? A guy like Guy—without ever thinking
such things—still might approach life that way,
taking it as it comes, right side up or right side
down. He hadn't been competing with Barnaby.
He was just being Guy.

Then one spring, with a late-season snow
dripping from his garage eaves and a few blue-
green buds on a lilac bush beside it, an old pickup
truck pulled into Barnaby's yard on Sunday
morning when he had just begun thinking about
the day's trip north. It was Lance.

"I thought I'd come see *you* for a change," said the boy, grinning and giving him a hug.

Everything changed after that, or maybe nothing had to change: it had been there all along, at the end of a long road winding over the horizon until it circled the earth. Here was Lance, and at last, here they were together.

TWO DISCOMFORTS MAKE A COMFORT

For a week, she'd had the almost welcome distraction of a persistent sorrow. She ate on one side of her mouth, fought an annoying tendency to count chews—which this encouraged for some reason—and hoarded her comfort away from a crumbling tooth till the morning of her dental appointment came. As luck would have it, this coincided with the arrival of a winter storm and provided yet another thing to bicker over.

Paul, her husband, said walking downtown to the dentist's office was silly with sleet pelting their breakfast nook window as it had in several salvoes minutes before she came downstairs to find him making toast. He believed in weather forecasts. She said they were impossible to take seriously when every storm front was treated like an air raid. This was one cause of the troubles they were having—the fact he could so easily believe, she so easily doubt.

He was taken in by appearances. He swallowed tall tales with the gusto of a child on a carnival midway. Just last week, he had purchased a vacuum cleaner from a door-to-door salesman who swore his magical machine could only be purchased this way. That evening, she found it online for a hundred dollars less. Of course it was petty of her and worse to tell him about it when it couldn't accomplish a thing beyond proving a point.

Paul shrugged. "The man has to live," he said. "Why bother to check it out?"

This was Paul's way, going through life avoiding, trusting, getting swindled, and shrugging, while keeping the whole while to a high road, at least where strangers were concerned. Even if they were wrong, strangers meant well. Even if they lied, it was only to survive.

Her, though? Here was another matter. He who trusted appearances suspected melodrama in her leaving the car at home to walk downtown, a mile at least.

"And a mile back," he said with the air of a self-satisfied accountant at the end of a fine calculation. "Anyway, I see what I see. You don't have to take the television's word for it." He pointed toward the window with a plastic spatula. This was a weak gesture since nothing much was happening outside at the moment, and the melted tip of the spatula curved toward the ceiling. Had her eyes followed it, they would have gone up to a dusty light fixture with a single dead fly cooking in its frosted globe.

"Don't take everything I do so personally," she said, not for the first time. "I'm not going off in a huff over us—I just feel like walking this morning."

"In this storm?"

They went on this way gingerly, as couples do when they've been bickering a lot, have learned too much about each other's moves, and so feel frightfully on their toes.

"Take the car," he persisted. "I'm not going anywhere, or I'll drive if you want and wait around for you." He had awoken this morning full of solicitude she couldn't believe. He had coffee poured, eggs cracked in a pan, and bread perched in toaster slots.

She wished with all her heart he did have

somewhere to go this morning —to a bar, to a mother he loved more than her, to a job he loved more than anything—so then she could understand why she was so glad to be leaving in a few minutes, savoring every minute of it by walking; why even a dentist would do for a destination; and why even a toothache felt good.

But this marriage of only three years had no lightning-bolt revelations, no cud of guilt for a therapist to chew and regurgitate in clots they could digest, nothing paramount to explain her wish to end it, which she maintained so constantly and deeply that the dull pain in her mouth week-long seemed its mere reverberation.

At times she thought she must be crazy.

"It has no logic," he argued against her suggestion they divorce. "We're getting along fine if you really think about it."

She *had* really thought about it, but each time he said this, she went dutifully back to it as to a church she no longer believed in. She thought it all through, again and again, with the same result. She felt like a dead fly baking in a frosted globe. Outside their kitchen window, a mauve November dawn had turned murky.

Paul stared at eggs in a skillet.

"Good old Paul," she hummed, joining him in

his contemplation of butter sizzling and snapping around edges of thickening egg white.

"It's got to be all of a mile from here."

"Give it up, Paul." She took the spatula from his hand.

He turned away, reached for an orange in a bowl, and glanced outside again. "Geez, it's early. Is this why we got up so early, so you could go walking in a storm?'

"You might have stayed in bed."

"And miss all this? Not for the world."

She was too accustomed to his bitter outbursts. She had lain awake before sunrise walking in her thoughts downtown to the professional building where upstairs over a greeting card shop her dentist had quarters with an optometrist, a chiropractor, and a law firm with two partners. She marked off the distance by familiar things along her way, pausing before each—as if before Stations of the Cross—the library, the bakeshop, and the bridge, not because she cared about any of it, but for the same reason bored travelers read dull books on long flights over the sea. It helped pass the time. In bed with Paul on nights like these, she had crossed many an ocean.

The late moon at their window dissolved in clouds of the approaching weather, a white tablet disintegrating in a glass of water. Finally she imagined herself having walked so far from home she no longer knew what things went with what streets or how many crossings there were either ahead of her or behind. Then the clock radio going off at seven flung her back to the man beside her….

Paul, standing once more over his eggs, pointed to her steaming cup. "Sit down," he said, "before it's cold."

Give up, she thought, *before it's dead, while yet there's some principle in leaving.*

The toast came up. He brought the eggs around.

"You're going out in this murk to think about us."

"No."

"Pure melodrama."

She felt herself slipping from a ledge. Behind her, slumped in their kitchen, sat Paul with his head in his hands.

She landed on her feet at the corner yard two streets away where a picket fence leaned and a spaniel yipped as she passed, and where on warm afternoons of the autumn as she walked to the library she had seen a baby sometimes sitting out on a blanket with a girl too young to be its mother. Sleet had resumed in salvoes. Taking no notice of her, the spaniel barked at a door. The eyes of the young girl could be seen peering between slats in a blind. Five corners later in front of the public library, a custodian in blue coveralls hauled down a flag he had raised but an hour before.

A line stood at the bakery counter as if pastries could be worn as ear muffs. Then, as the bridge fog curled through girders below her, coalescing at the point of a sandbar, the ice, which had melted elsewhere so far, coated everything here. She clung to an iron railing with her bare hand till her fingers grew numb, and then she cradled the railing between her coat sleeve and side, inching along toward wet pavement on the other side. Cars crept past. She skirted a state university campus where Paul, a young prof., taught mostly in the evening division.

Her dentist awaiting her looked eager as the spaniel. On account of the bad weather and cancellations in his appointment book, he had given both his receptionist and his assistant the day off. He sat at the receptionist's desk reading a newspaper.

"Ah," he said, looking up. "I wondered if you

were coming, so I called your husband. He told me you were on your way. And the streets?"

"Not bad on the whole." She said nothing about the bridge. *Why did he have to bring Paul into it?*

Long after she had settled into his patient's chair—adjusted so far back she seemed to be lying on a gentle slope with her feet pointed uphill, while Novocain was yet creeping along her jawbone—out in the reception room her coat on a wooden tree dripped melted ice in near syncopation with a clock ticking. Outside, the air had turned from gray to gauzy white. Buildings across the street slipped in and out of view.

From somewhere she recalled this textbook paradox which ran through her mind like a song lyric she picked up and couldn't get rid of and could never herself sing since its words died on her tongue.

> *Here is a desert. Take one grain of sand away, and here is still a desert. Take another away, and it is still a desert. Take millions away one by one, and the desert remains. So a desert—*

Yet this is wrong, she said to herself, for here

is sand, and this is a desert. Neither do ice pellets and snowflakes make a storm, yet outside was the storm Paul predicted.

The slope fell away beneath her.

"That should take care of things," said the dentist. "Not many years ago, you would have lost that tooth. Today, we can save things we couldn't save then."

How strangely such words resonate at times like these, as if echoes within echoes. One carries them about and hears them again in dreams, ripped from their context and pasted into another. They are discovered again on the sides of passing boxcars while one waits at a signal crossing.

We can save things today we couldn't save then. Perhaps what passed for the world's wisdom was merely this, a collusion of the deities Longing, Grief, and Chance-Remark.

Here was another: *"You can hardly see outside,"* said the dentist by way of goodbye as he glanced over her shoulder.

She knew all about it, having lived it every day. She mumbled a thank you from lips like flapping carton lids, and left with her coat over her arm.

Downstairs in the card shop opposite a side

entrance from the elevator, she finished buttoning her coat in front of a section labeled *Condolence and Loss*, mostly flowers and those mostly lilies bannered with regrets. As she struggled with an unfamiliar collar button, a familiar knit hat bobbed into view. Paul, who hadn't yet noticed her, stood the other side of the display, dripping in what of course had to be *Friendship and Love.*

His manner suggested he was deliberately there searching for the right words, though of course she knew better, for Paul always had the right words, and kept them easily at hand.

He had come downtown to meet her, even if his manner at the moment suggested he was shopping. So convincing he was, she might have slipped away unnoticed but for the chance of a card falling from his fingers, skittering underneath toward her foot, and revealing a familiar shoe as he bent to retrieve it. So there they were for a second, his hand groping for the card resting upon her foot, ridiculous enough that they both actually laughed in unabashed unison, despite the Novocain, despite the lowering sky, despite everything.

In any other story, it might have been the beginning, the sort of tale readymade for one's children when they asked how you and Dad met. "If I hadn't kept my dental appointment that day, if he hadn't wandered in out of the storm to find a birthday card for an old friend, you wouldn't be here today."

That's how things went. But for the household gods, none of us would be here today.

He loped around to her side. "You needn't have come down here," she said. "I didn't need a ride home."

He hadn't brought the car. He'd walked in the storm.

"Pure melodrama," she murmured.

He shrugged. "When nothing else will do, I guess, and I brought your gloves—you'll need them in this."

He helped her with her reluctant collar button. Turning aside for a second, he stooped to retrieve the fallen card which he stuffed in among condolences, but not before she saw it, an hourglass with tiny hearts sifting through as sand. *To my love for all time.*

She wanted to laugh and she wanted to cry. He looked so forlorn and also so noble with snow water running down his face where tears might have been. He looked so hapless and yet so heroic. She might have been seeing him for the first time or for the last. For an instant their eyes met.

Anyone looking after them would have given up when they were no farther than the next street north. The dentist in fact had been looking out from a window up above. Trudging toward the bridge and the university, they slipped from his view. By then it was snowing most heavily.

"When we get as far as my office," shouted Paul through wind and a coat collar zipped up to his nose, "we'll stop and warm up. I'll make tea."

She couldn't possibly have heard with a city snowplow just then passing, spewing salt-sand from its underbelly. She was thinking about all those hearts in the hourglass, the ones having fallen, the others on their way, like grains of sand, like ice pellets and snowflakes.

MISSING PERSONS

*G*reat explorers should have been sent looking for Margaret's happiness, so remote it seemed whenever she tried to find it. Perhaps it would be found over the next ridge of a remarkable mountain range, yet Margaret sensed her happiness was at the end of a trek of desolate hills where only the luck of a hero might bring you.

After sticking it out for nineteen years, she'd hoped to name her husband Jesse Robins as the source of her contentment. Having raised a daughter Sarah, she found instead that Jesse was a hopeless drunk, and named him in a divorce suit.

A matter of days before this came to final court, she went to Sarah's high school graduation in a suburban Minneapolis auditorium. She, at least, would heed a parent's call to the big occasions in a child's life, and—this seemed cruel—she felt as if she had to atone, as if she was the guilty one, not Jesse, who wouldn't bother showing up and was probably out of his mind in a bar this very minute.

She took a taxi from the apartment where she had lived the two months since leaving him, and in her eagerness to do the right thing, she arrived before the stage was lit. The speaker's podium, hung with a bow of school colors, had just been shoved out from a wing. An usher went up one side and down the other opening high windows with a sash pole. Margaret sat near the front so Sarah might by chance see her. The girl needed whatever reassurance that would bring. She needed to know that at least one of them was here to witness this occasion.

"Thank God," said Margaret, "this isn't her wedding day."

Sarah had been more affected by the impending divorce than her mother could have foreseen. All those years, she stayed with Jesse waiting for the day Sarah would be grown up enough and understand enough to be less affected. Whoever said, *Wait till the kids are grown up?* What a folly that seemed now. Life slipped away, all those wasted years, to have this much heartache at the end of it and to feel guilty regardless.

Hadn't Sarah deplored her father's drinking also? Hadn't she complained as bitterly when he upset their every plan, when he embarrassed her in front of friends, and whenever he broke a glass or tripped over the dog's dish in the middle of the night waking them both with his garbled cursing?

"If only we could live like normal people," Sarah must have said a thousand times.

Margaret had yet to recover from hearing her say that she wouldn't take sides now that it had come to a divorce, that she thought it all wrong, that both of them were to blame.

Behind her, gradually, the echoing spaces of the auditorium filled, the distant talk of a few people discussing the weather became the general hum of the many. Margaret felt relieved of her sense of being conspicuously alone in a very large place, convicted and awaiting her sentence. Then a drum rolled, two trumpets sang out from a doorway, and the graduating class marched in two by two. Margaret twisted in her chair to catch a glimpse of Sarah whom she missed regardless since the girl was one of the first in the march and so had gone past her by the time she looked.

What followed, predictably, was one of those occasions that blur almost the instant after they come into focus. It might have been a wedding after all, or somebody's funeral, or a large family reunion where there are too many faces, and a mixture of small talk, declarations, and emotion that leave a person feeling frayed.

Filing out afterwards in the daze such times induce, Margaret heard her name called and gasped so audibly that a man in front of her turned around to see what the matter was. Sarah's grandmother was hailing her from a row of folding chairs set up in the rear for those who arrived late. Beside her, a gray lump, sat Jesse whom she had spoken to twice by phone and not seen at all since a sheriff's deputy had served him with a divorce complaint and a judge's protection order which of course couldn't be expected to keep him from his own daughter's graduation; Margaret had counted on his bad habits to accomplish that.

Grandma Robins was the first to greet her. "We were about the last ones in the door, but we made it," she chirped. "Wasn't that graduation speech a dandy? I should say so, filled with memorable things," she continued, leaping into the void since Margaret couldn't claim to have noticed the speech, couldn't have said whether it was a long speech or a short one, and was too dumbfounded to answer her regardless.

The old lady took her arm, though it hadn't been offered. She was a busy little woman, always overdressed and fussy about herself as a preening bird, with her dark hair belying her seventy-nine years and her rouge in all the wrong places.

Rising from his chair at last, with his shoulders seeming to drag the rest of him along, Jesse said, "Hullo, Maggie." He had been drunk and remembered nothing of her two phone calls, so he thought these his first words with her since she left him. He tried to smile, and when she didn't, he stared at his shoes.

Jesse's most obvious disadvantage after an alcoholic decade was the potbelly hanging from his lanky frame like a bag of slim pickings. His hair had been brushed without the help of a mirror, making its disorder, considered on a global scale, more that of world wars than isolated skirmishes, exactly the disorder of his mind, groomed likewise without looking at himself. His part formed a cowlick waggling into space. His mind formed thoughts that appeared without prelude in the wrong place and never attached themselves to anything else.

He had come off a nine-week drinking binge —not for the sake of divorce proceedings, which he had done his best to ignore, but for Sarah's graduation—but not so far off that he wasn't a lurching, shaking, hung-over wreck.

Grandma Robins' hold on Margaret's arm turned into an embrace, and then back into an arm hold while she used her free hand to steady her son as the three of them walked out through double doors flung open to the dewy light and warm fragrances of a nearly summer evening.

"I was just saying to Jesse that I knew if we waited here long enough, you would come by, Maggie, and we could all go out together and be with our Sarah on her big day. Won't she be happy!"

They worked their way down some stone stairs in the throng. Now that she had them to-gether, Grandma Robins seemed unable to let go of either, though the press of the crowd some-times had them all on different steps, and she would be pulled down on one side to keep hold of Margaret, and then pulled up on the other by Jesse trailing them from the step above. If sheer physical contortion might have mended a busted marriage, her efforts would have done the trick, but the only certain result when they at last stood together on a grassy patch below was that she felt a stitch in her side, and her corsage had been knocked cockeyed.

"Jesse, what a laggard you've become," she scolded with her fingers fretting the gardenia mound on her breast. "Do I look straight again, Maggie?"

"You look fine, Grandma." Margaret had assumed the false nonchalance of one who has recovered sufficiently from a surprise to attempt concealing it.

"God knows, I always try to look good no matter how old I get. I just can't abide people who use their years as an excuse for neglecting themselves." This seemed intended for the benefit of her son who at forty-seven could have been mistaken for sixty.

Margaret nodded without knowing why.

Jesse worked his face into several patterns of wrinkles while darting glances between the sod and the sky. Dandelions winked in the sod, small white clouds in the sky. While the two women talked, and he waited hungrily for his wife to notice him and say something, he sullenly surveyed the crowd around them, itself having broken up into clusters such as theirs.

In the center of one such, larger than the others, stood the commencement speaker, a humorist named Jake Leary, autographing commencement programs and making agreeable responses to those coming forward to congratulate him on his excellent address and hilarious humor column. *As numberless as stars in the heavens were opportunities,* he had said, though in words more original and worthier of the attention in which he now basked. Jesse found himself in deep shadow with the sun setting between buildings beyond a grove of slender pines. The humor columnist, who was about Jesse's age, stood squarely in the ruddy light of a vagrant beam as if heaven conspired his triumph. Jesse, in eclipse, scowled, squinted at the bright celebrity, knew himself a failure.

The cluster of Margaret, his mother, and himself was the smallest and most peculiar, for though it had the three of them, and family therefore, it had no friends and as yet no graduate in cap and gown. They awaited Sarah with cameras pointing all around them and other clusters dissolving and coalescing in new poses. Blackbirds clucked from trees across the street. Pigeons cooed from ledges of the auditorium. It was the sort of evening to offer a sense of the world's enlargement, an evening of prospects suddenly opened onto vistas of shadow-splashed lawn, an evening of shirtsleeves and interlocking arms.

No wonder normally shy people pushed through the crowd to shake the humorist's hand. No wonder he was hugged by a woman with plum-colored hair. Nature sustained his hopeful view of life. And Jesse, seeing for himself no prospects whatsoever, with his head aching and his arms in soiled shirtsleeves, squinted and scowled the more and resented everything around him, most of all the humorist.

Laughter, chat, and bird chirp flitted near and then far away. Hopes might have soared to a sky turning azure with an evening star glimmering in it. Jesse resented all of this without exception. Mistaking the evening star for an airplane, he did not resent heavenly bodies but people with the freedom and means to fly away. He himself felt heavy and too earthbound to be lofted skyward by any human device. He shoved the toes of his wingtip oxfords into nests of grass tuft and dandelion frond dense enough to hide their scuffs— not that he cared what anyone saw of him or what they thought if they bothered to look, nor that he cared what his mother thought who must have had him in mind when she spoke of people neglecting themselves.

She shrieked just then. "Jesse, your socks don't even match!"

It was true, they didn't. Not even close, for one was a light blue and the other an argyle of lemon diamonds over brown, and Jesse wasn't surprised, having put them on that way. He hitched up his trouser legs and snorted his disdain of matching socks for all the world—Margaret mostly—to witness. He staggered through a rose bush.

His mother bawled that family quarrels in public shamed her, Jesse's neglect of himself shamed her, this divorce shamed her. A dam had burst within the old woman, and she repeated these things louder still till she noticed that her son's strange dance and her outbursts were attracting attention. Jesse hopped from the rose bush with his pants cuff torn. Nearer clusters fanned out, glancing over shoulders, and eased away. Jesse quieted.

Freed at last from Grandma's grip, Margaret herself stepped a stride away, did her best to ignore both of them, and scanned the crowd for Sarah. She feared the worst. A half hour passed without her showing up. A distant church bell began the chime of its vesper song. Shadows enlarged and thickened into darkness.

Who knows where the multitudes of such occasions go, how they slip away like time itself. The three waited. A coat lifted off the forearm to be put on again against the freshening breeze, a camera dropped into a handbag, somewhere a door slammed and a car started, the popular humorist assumed into heaven with his plum-haired woman, and a thousand people become three isolated in what seems a wink. And still no sign of the one the three of them awaited.

Jesse's eyes swam. His mouth screwed open in the blotchy round of his face. He spoke as if some light of their own sad spectacle dawned in him as the sun's light went out. "Maggie. Oh why, Maggie?" was the most he could manage to say, and he didn't know whether he meant *why* has our daughter abandoned us, or *why* are you leaving me, or *why* are some men successful and I such a failure.

Margaret answered only the first. "If she didn't know you would be here, you could hardly expect her to look for you afterwards."

She didn't herself find this satisfactory, since Sarah knew she would be there and apparently hadn't looked for her either, but this explanation seemed enough for Jesse who found in it at last and at least what he had most come here for—a word, albeit a caustic word, and a look of recognition, albeit a look of disdain, from his wife. The truth, which she and perhaps he as well had finally guessed, she hadn't the heart to say nor he the heart to hear, that their daughter must have seen them all waiting for her and run away rather than face this mockery of a family.

Grandma was less forgiving. "I know she was here," she whined. "I heard her name called. Is this what we deserve for coming to her graduation?"

"I saw her cross the stage and get her diploma —she was lovely," Margaret said defiantly as she turned her back on them and strode off to find her car.

Jesse's ears rang. He bowed his head. A chill creeping out of the auditorium stones enveloped his ankles.

Next morning, a tearful Sarah tried explaining herself to her mother who had phoned her at eight and invited her to a coffee shop in a strip mall five blocks from home.

"I shouldn't have done it," said Sarah, "but it seems like I no longer have a family."

"You're wrong, you have all of us still. With time you will see this."

But for a long time after Sarah finished crying and finished her English muffin and tea and went back home, not even her mother could see so far.

After the divorce, Margaret moved to California where friends helped her get settled and gave her advice about the new hair style that so often marks a passage and a transition.

Jesse didn't deliberately grow a beard: he just quit shaving for several months, a hit and miss affair with him anyway. The haphazard result favored him sufficiently that he soon found a female friend who was no more partial to sobriety than he was.

Grandma Robins had a stroke, but to her credit waited long enough to have it that nobody saw the point of blaming the divorce for putting her in a nursing home.

Sarah might have joined her mother in California, but stayed behind for the same reason her mother went.

"My friends," she said, "my life."

"Your choice, not your life," said her mother. "Your life is wherever you are—it always comes with you."

So it was for them all.

AND THE DOG CAME BACK

*G*eorge Cobb left the Purple Palace Nightclub after his usual two after-work martinis. Inspiration mingled with intoxication, a sudden jolt of natural daylight, the freshening scent of an autumn rainfall, and concern about a kid named Jude.

As he made his way across a parking lot to his construction company's dump truck, he noticed a man sitting under an umbrella facing the main north-south thoroughfare through Twin Rivers, George's route home. At the man's back was the derelict Paradise Hotel looking more than ever sinister with the long shadows of late afternoon upon it. George's company had been awarded a contract for demolishing the hotel. Had he not been surveying the scene with its daunting challenges in mind, the man under the umbrella might have gone unnoticed.

Alongside, a small black dog with white ears sat on a battered suitcase as if posing for a travel agency advertisement. George had the feeling he had seen this dog somewhere before. The umbrella was sheltering the man from a shower of the late October sort that might turn to snow overnight. The dog was sitting in the rain.

Minutes later, George owned the dog.

It was not exactly an impulse purchase, but yet another instance of George's notions about how strange and coincidental life at times could be. Moments before at the bar, he had asked an acquaintance seated next to him his opinion of breeds making both a good watchdog and a good companion animal. This had led to discussions up and down the bar producing dog stories supporting opinions as various as Rottweilers and Jack Russell terriers with socialized pit bulls somewhere in between.

In fact the discussion was still going on in George's absence. No breed up to that point resembled the dog George was about to buy, no breed anywhere.

"It breaks my heart even to think about selling this old friend," said the man under the umbrella as he began something resembling an adoption agency interview:

Where did George live?

"Between here and Paradise Park," said George, pointing to his left, which happened to be north.

"Halfway between would you say?"

"About two-thirds," said George.

"That would make it about eight miles from here."

"Six point five on the nose," said George. "I drive it five times some days. I ought to know."

"A few curves in that highway as I recall?"

"A few, yes. It goes around some marshes."

"Been living there long?"

"Twenty years," said George.

"Just you?"

"Me and my wife," said George.

"Any kids?"

"Just the two of us, Phyllis and me."

"No other dog?"

"None."

"If you like dogs and mean to give this one a good home, you'll have to let him run now and then."

"Why not? We live in the country."

"Floyd likes to run," said the man, patting the wet forehead of the dog. "He likes to chase rabbits. Any rabbits around your place?"

"Lots of squirrels, but I haven't seen any rabbits for a while."

"Floyd likes to chase squirrels too."

"Will you let him loose to chase squirrels now and then?"

"Why not?" said George.

"Your wife too—she'll let him loose?"

"Why not?" said George.

Of course, he planned to give the dog to Jude Henley, but so far nothing he said had been exactly a lie. After all, Paradise Park had squirrels. The boy would let him run. There were no other dogs in the mostly vacant park, none until next summer's tourist season, far enough away to seem forever.

The man under the umbrella scratched his head under a baseball cap. He then scratched the dog's head as if the two of them had to think about it. George scratched his head. After the conclusion of this itchy contagion came a decisive sigh sufficient to send a small cloud into the chilly autumn air.

"What do you say, Floyd, old boy? Is this so long, old friend?"

As if on cue, Floyd sat bolt upright and raised his front legs with neatly folded paws, executing what might have clinched the grand prize in a national dog show.

"That will be fifty dollars," said the man under the umbrella. "Though it breaks my heart to let go of Floyd at any price."

The interview thus ended with George fishing a fifty from his wallet.

The man under the umbrella held it up to a streetlight to check for watermarks. "You can't be too careful about these larger bills," he said. "Counterfeits are going around."

From George's viewpoint, his fifty was an investment. Phyllis would worry less about Jude and his mother living alone, a half mile from any help. Jude needed a companion. They both needed a watchdog. Even this little mongrel would do.

Floyd's shiny coat was entirely black except for snow-white ears upright and flopped over halfway, suggesting he was both amiable and alert. He cocked his head to one side and appeared to be thinking things over while his sale was completed.

With those two after-work drinks firing his imagination George right off renamed him *Archie*.

"Come on, Archie," said George.

"Goodbye, Floyd," said the man under the umbrella.

Floyd Archie trotted after George as if they were old friends united.

By this time, George was as wet as the dog. When he opened the dump truck's passenger door, Archie jumped in as if he had spent a lifetime riding in construction company dump trucks. During the six point five mile ride to his new home in country north of Twin Rivers, he sat up in the front seat and stared through the windshield with the easy nonchalance of people like George making the trip every day. He did not even shake to dry off his coat as dogs will usually do first chance.

Noting these things, George was certain he had purchased an exceptional animal.

On the way out of Twin Rivers, he bought a twenty-five-pound bag of dog chow. He called Phyllis who had already invited Kate and Jude to visit the next afternoon. After an overnight, Archie would meet his new owners.

It was bound to be a surprise.

Archie barked as George turned from the highway six point five miles north of Twin Rivers. The dump truck in low gear, gradually ascended the long driveway up a hillside where his split-level ranch house sprawled in a grove of burr oaks. On the descent to its right were rows of sheds, a fleet of pea-green construction machines, more dump trucks, and Phyllis's orange school bus parked in its usual spot with its nose pointed out toward tomorrow's school day.

"We're home," said George.

Archie jumped out and headed straight to the house as Phyllis glanced from a kitchen window. George wondered how this could all seem so normal. The three—George, Phyllis, and Archie—could be imagined having done this in a previous life.

After dinner Phyllis and George settled into their usual living room spots. Archie found a spot on Phyllis' lap.

(Half-serious bickering had become the main game in the Cobb approach to marriage, Phyllis pretending to be angry and George pretending to be defensive. Only the dog was in the dark—along with others within earshot year after year long before Archie came into their lives. Everyone knowing them had long been amazed at the durability of a marriage always seeming to be teetering on the edge of fisticuffs.)

At the moment, Archie was licking Phyllis' hands, recently in cookie dough needing to chill an hour or so. Somehow a mixed-breed lapdog in love with cookie dough was supposed to protect Kate and Jude in their isolated home.

"Well nothing is going to happen anyway," said George.

"You can't be so sure with the landlord gone to Florida till next spring." Phyllis rubbed one of Archie's ears. "I don't know how much good this adorable little fellow would be if anything happened."

"The guy I bought him from says he likes to chase rabbits."

"It's not rabbits I'm worried about, George. I can hardly sleep thinking about it, and I need my rest to drive that school bus five days a week. I stopped in to chat with Kate this afternoon. Jude wasn't around. He had gone through the park to check on the cabin on the far end where that unemployed singer is staying. Would you believe that bullying landlord is making the kid go up there every day just to see if she hasn't skipped out without paying her rent? Pretty soon it will be dark after school. What's Jude supposed to do then?"

At that point, as if to reassure Phyllis, Archie leaped away to a living room window, and with his paws upon its sill, began barking.

"What did I tell you," said George, "Archie is a first rate watchdog. Jude can bring Archie with him after dark. I'll buy Jude a good flashlight."

George disappeared into an entryway and returned after turning on a battery of floodlights illuminating everything Cobb Construction within a quarter mile.

"Nothing out there that I can see," he said at last. "I'm not sure why Archie is barking."

Meantime, Archie, running to yet another window, was paws up growling on that one.

"He must be hearing something," said George.

"Great," said Phyllis. "Just what Kate and Jude need: a dog who either hallucinates or has a rich imagination."

This was but the beginning.

Archie seemed to have been programmed to undergo multiple personality transformations after an elapsed time, in this instance about four hours from the moment George had purchased him. Throughout what remained of the evening and into the night he was not the same dog, but, in stages, more like several dogs. He seemed to pass through fits of schizophrenia and bi-polarity, morose and begging for attention one minute, whining while lying down the next, and otherwise running around in circles near every door and window of the Cobb house of three levels.

In less than an hour, Archie had traipsed through rooms and barked from windows George had not gazed from all year. Betweentimes, he jumped up to lick the nearest available face and eat cookies caught in midair, a remarkable feat given the dog's size and the weight and density of Phyllis's molasses crinkles.

"I should have put some marijuana in them," said Phyllis.

She did not have that particular ingredient, but harbored a suspicion that George sometimes smoked a joint when safely out of the way in his construction company workshop. It was as good a moment as any to see if he would come clean. That failing, she began to wonder out loud if Archie was in the early stages of rabies. George of course dismissed this theory for no better reason than Phyllis was the first to think of it. Regardless, he went into the nearest bathroom and washed his hands and face. He kept his hands in his pockets the rest of the evening whenever Archie was anywhere near.

An alternative theory was needed.

"I think he just wants to chase rabbits," said George, recalling the words of Archie's former owner.

"In that case, George, maybe you should buy him a few rabbits, and let them run around in here. Maybe then I could sleep."

In bed by this time, they both stared at the ceiling while Archie still roamed. At five-minute intervals he would flash by in the hallway outside their room. Then he bounded in and ran across the foot of their bed.

Phyllis sat up and screamed. "George, you have to do something."

'Something' in this case was confining Archie to their three-car garage where when he wasn't knocking over paint cans and chewing holes in work gloves, he was flinging himself against its doors. This incessant banging kept even George awake.

Sometime after midnight, George—sporting purple plaid pajamas—tied Archie outside to a distant tree where he barked, yipped, yapped, and sometimes howled till exhaustion set in just as the moon lowered behind the most distant of Cobb Construction machinery sheds..

When he began barking again at sunrise, George, still in his pajamas, led him further downhill and tied him to the dump bucket of a gigantic pea-green loader. For a few seconds, he toyed with the idea of starting this monster and running its steel tracks over Archie, not just once, but back and forth several times to make sure. At least, this far from the house, the dog's endless barking could only be heard from front rooms.

"Why don't you just let him run?" said Phyllis as George returned with his latest report.

"I'm afraid he will run off and get lost."

"That's my hope," said Phyllis. ""I'm sure your newfound friend will not work out for Jude and Kate," she said. "They'd be better off with a hyena."

"He'll settle down once he gets to his new home and meets his new owners," said George, no longer himself convinced. "Anyway he cost fifty dollars, and what will we do with all the dog food?"

"You can have it for dinner the days you're late getting home."

An hour later, at the beginning of the Cobb Construction workday, George tossed a bit of ridicule Archie's way as he passed him on his way to a dump truck.

"Yip, yap, yap, yap, yip," said George.

"Yip, yap, yap, yap, yip, yip," replied Archie who threw in an extra yip and growl for good measure, none of this very convincing since simultaneously he had in his teeth the chain tethering him to the loader. At that point, George was by far the more convincing canine.

Phyllis fortunately missed this duel as she had driven off on her school bus route, intending to stay away all day, working around the St. Callixtus food shelf and soup kitchen, and possibly catching a nap betweentimes on the bus's bench seats.

When she returned at day's end with Kate and Jude in her otherwise empty bus, George had already moved Archie and tethered him to a burr oak near a redwood deck. The dog, perhaps from so much barking, had lost its vocal powers. In a gesture of friendliness as Kate and Jude approached, he even wagged his tail. Neither noticed that his chain tether was as taught as a piano wire.

George had just been sharing with Jude his thoughts about the value of taking people at their word—Archie's previous owner, rabbits, and the dog's amiable temperament were wistful examples.

"I named him Archie, just to get started, but you can give him any name you want. That was just for starters."

Jude was about to mention that he thought he had seen the same dog around Twin Rivers.

Phyllis was about to fill tumblers with apple cider.

George had almost arrived at the point of once again feeling good about everything.

Kate bent over to pat Archie's head. She would be glad she averted her face to hear something about rabbits George had just said to Jude. Archie picked that moment to execute an airborne, gymnastic pirouette, perhaps thinking he was about to be set free. This move would have earned him at least honorable mention in the annals of dog acrobatics had not his chain tether gotten in the way. When he came to earth in the resulting tangle of fur, flesh and chain links, Kate had inch-long parallel gashes on her wrist where blood was pooling.

After a pause of the sort following thunderclaps, Phyllis screamed for the second time in less than twenty-four hours. George leaped over a deck railing to do something rash and, on second guess, foolish. He opened the clasp on the tether. Archie might have planned it this way. Perhaps he meant no harm, but only wanted to be free.

The fifty-dollar dog immediately ran off apparently in search of rabbits. Jude ran after the dog without quite knowing why. George ran after Jude hollering profanities, some seldom heard even on construction sites from the most veteran of profaners.

Archie began well out front and increased his lead by the second. Over a hill, across a wild meadow recently mowed for hay, over yet another hill and through a valley or two. George gave up at the top of the first hill, Jude after two more hills, two valleys and a neighbor's ornamental duck pond. Archie would have outrun a greyhound in full stride, even with pausing on his merry way to catch his breath and throttle the neighbor's crested Peking duck. Then he disappeared entirely.

Jude found George on a tree stump catching his breath.

"I'm afraid I lost him, George."

"No matter. Good riddance to bad rubbish," said George, not foreseeing how his hobby farm neighbor would bill him for a hundred dollar duck and threaten to sue.

Meanwhile in Twin Rivers, an emergency room physician applying stitches brought up the possibility of rabies and a series of painful shots beginning soon if the dog was not found in time.

"Rabies! I told you so!" bellowed Phyllis when she confronted George at home, "*Your* damned mongrel Floyd needs an *exorcist*."

For a convert, Phyllis had obscure Catholic terminology remarkably at her disposal. Archie had become exclusively George's again. His name was changing back to Floyd.

No question of ownership or the supernatural delayed George. With Jude riding alongside in a Cobb Construction truck, he scoured every county highway, tree farm trail, logging road, bridle path, and gully within five miles. Phyllis and Kate made posters featuring pictures of Archie AKA Floyd and Floyd AKA Archie. Jude and George tacked them to community bulletin boards as far away as Paradise Park. Every Cobb construction crew was on lookout even as concrete was poured and backhoes dug trenches

After five days without Archie and the same number without his vodka martinis, George pulled into the Purple Palace parking lot. When he climbed out of his dump truck, he heard a familiar bark. Nearby under what passed for a shade tree sat Archie on a busted and beaten up grip just as before. In a lawn chair sat his owner from the days Archie was Floyd just as before.

"My god," said George to the man in the lawn chair. "How long has he been here?

"Never left," said the other. "He's been here since he was a pup. Been looking to sell him."

"I bought him almost two weeks ago," said George. "Paid fifty bucks."

"A bargain that nearly broke my heart, but that was a different dog," said the man.

At this point Floyd Archie was wagging his tail and licking George's hand. When he once again thought of rabies, George put both hands in his construction coveralls.

"Nice to see you, Archie, old boy," said George. "You can come with me to the vet now."

"That will be seventy-five bucks," said the man. "Not the same dog."

"Rabies," said George. "He bit a family friend."

"You're breaking my heart," said the man putting a hand in that spot over his plaid shirt. "Seventy-five, no checks."

George could not dicker or dither with rabies in the picture, but he had only two fives in his wallet.

"Be back in a minute," he said. "Don't go anywhere with that dog."

"First come, first served," said the man in the lawn chair. "I can't guarantee someone else won't buy him before you get back."

"I'll beat any offer," said George.

"You're breaking my heart."

Had he not been so intent on rabies and cashing a check under Dusty Dwyer's countersignature, he might have thought for the umpteenth time, *life is sure strange, all sides of it.*

Dusty detected something amusing in George's story.

"Nobody ever made money by trusting people," he said. "That old crook used to be a scrap iron merchant. Ask me about it sometime."

"What about now?"

"Not now, *one of these days.* You'd want to kill him on the spot. Murder, even off my property— in front of that hotel or near the church—could damage my good reputation."

"Your good reputation?"

"Yea, George, you're a businessman. You know what I mean. I can't be too careful. Murder can happen anywhere, and it's bad for appearances."

The former scrap iron merchant pocketed seventy-five plus ten for the dog's leash.

"Be sure to let Wilson run now and then. He loves to run just like the one you had—from the same litter, the last one. It breaks my heart so see him go."

"Wilson?"

"That's his name. I thought I mentioned it earlier."

"Come on, Archie," said George. "Next stop is the vet's."

"Goodbye, Wilson. You're breaking my heart."

At the veterinarian's, two options lay straight ahead for Floyd Archie Wilson whose name was now longer than most university presidents, and sounded like something from an FBI *most wanted* list.

The dog responsible for all this could either be executed so his brain might be examined, or held for ten days to see if he got sick and died. George called Phyllis. Phyllis said she would check with Kate. While George waited, he read his way through a stack of magazines with titles like *Dog World, Cat Lover,* and *Horse and Pony* in which he learned among other things how to tell a horse from a pony. This turned out to be more than a matter of size.

About the same time George was learning that ponies usually have thicker manes than horses,

Phyllis' school bus pulled into the St. Callixtus Church parking lot. For the moment, rabies and a slowly-healing dog bite had overtaken her parish volunteer duties. She had not come to work, but to pray for guidance.

George favored brain surgery.

Phyllis wavered after consulting one of several *Lives of Saints* in a small parish library. St. Roch, patron saint of dogs and dog-owners, straddled all sides of the debate. He was also patron saint of surgeons—presumably even brain surgeons—and fighters of pestilence, presumably including rabies. It didn't stop there: he was patron of the falsely accused, of gravediggers, of secondhand dealers like the one who sold Floyd, and of gullible idiots like George. In a state of hopeless, supernatural confusion, Phyllis dithered.

Jude did not have a vote, but his views took him rambling once again over terrain between the Cobb's back deck and the neighbor's ornamental duck pond. Setting aside a crested Peking capsized in the middle of it, Archie's had been an awesome run.

It struck all of them as foolish to take chances, but nevertheless, something else was in the air.

Kate had at first abstained on grounds of self-interest and her faith in things happening for the best in the long run. Ten days would still give her a one-day margin.

"If anything happens, I know Jude will be in good hands," she said.

Phyllis nodded assurance while thinking of Jude growing up with more homemade cookies than any human could possible digest.

Kate voted for Floyd Archie, and she had been the one with veto power. At that point Phyllis called George on her cell phone.

Ponies also were more barrel-shaped than horses.

Floyd Archie Wilson won a stay of execution and then a reprieve.

Ten days of room-and-board at the vet's, plus an array of tests brought George's bill to a few cents less than two thousand dollars. Given the dog's certificate of good health and George's burgeoning investment, one might have thought he would take it home for use as a guard dog in his far flung construction machinery sheds. By this time he had learned how pointless that plan would turn out to be. Instead he held the vet's office door wide open, releasing Floyd Archie Wilson who flew off in the general direction of yet another name and further sales by the iron merchant.

The vet's receptionist, witnessing all this, spoke up for the first time.

"I've seen him in here before, maybe at least ten times with ten different owners, mostly tourists. You can't mistake a black dog with snow-white ears. Only one I have ever seen. Each time he gets a full set of vaccinations and a check-up. Each time he has a different name and gets a new computer file. What with all his rabies shots, it's a wonder he hasn't exploded. I sometimes wonder if he's not a homing dog."

"Homing?"

"You know, like one of those pigeons that always find their way back and carry messages. Either that or he imprints on certain people for certain reasons we can only guess, but we can't take chances, so every time he shows up here, he gets all the shots. We don't say anything. Lawsuits, you know."

"A pigeon? Messages? Imprints? Lawsuits?

George should have known: Floyd Archie Wilson had become a local industry, probably circulating more money than most Chamber of Commerce members. George shrugged and walked out, more than ever convinced that life was strange, all sides of it.

Every year after that, he received in the mail a

notice that his dog was due for his annual check-up. Every year he received a birthday card addressed to his home, not on his birthday, but his dog's. The vet was a marketing genius. The retired scrap iron merchant was an entrepreneur. Floyd Archie Wilson was the most remarkable dog since Lassie came home.

George was the pigeon for now.

ABOUT THE AUTHOR

James Casper has been writing ever since he was the editor of *The Loyolan*, his high school newspaper. A veteran writer now in his 8th decade, he continues to produce tastefully written novels, spellbinding short stories, and thought-provoking essays.

James was born and grew up in southern Minnesota. Apart from living in various Minnesota locales, he has resided in Boston, St. Louis, eastern Tennessee, and London, England where he finds inspiration walking along the Thames with Kate, his wife of many years. Traveling across the U.S. and Europe and writing all the while, he is most at home working at his laptop (formerly his Olympia typewriter) capturing thoughts, getting to know characters, and spinning tales that fascinate this peripatetic writer. He hopes his efforts bring you many pleasant hours of reading and reflection.

ALSO BY JAMES CASPER

An Accidental Pope: A Mystery in Five Boxes

Everywhere in Chains: Secrets of the North Shore

(and its Polish translation, Listy do Penelope)

The Far End of the Park

Turning Wind Tales: Reservation Stories

The Zodiac Club: A Constellation of Stories

Three Hundred Years in the Life of a Family

www.ingramcontent.com/pod-product-compliance
Lightning Source LLC
Chambersburg PA
CBHW050944120626
46552CB00001B/377